THE ROOF

—.—

A NOVEL

NYK BROWNSILVA

Copyright © 2023 by Nyk Brownsilva

First edition 2023

Cove design by- Ivanol Lagos for paperback/ hardcover Ashley Santoro for the digital

ISBN, paperback: 979-8-9881333-0-8

ISBN:, hardcover: 979-8-9881333-1-5

ISBN, digital: 979-8-9881333-2-2

Published by: Amazon.com/ Barns n Noble press/LuLu press/Kobo

For my mom

If she could only see me now.

1

CATS AND DOGS

Love is supposed to be an intense affection for another person. Yet in this moment, Jack feels nothing but the warm sand on his toes. *A long walk on the beach. How has my life ended up in a cliché?* he thinks, looking at the girl that declares herself his girlfriend. She is droning on about nothing that interests Jack. *Jessica can sure talk about nothing. Dammit, Jack, concentrate!* The argument in his head continues as he smiles at the tiny redhead clinging to his arm like it's her property. She is petite, but she has a monster grip.

Jessica is a clingy girlfriend, something Jack has not experienced with other women he'd been with. However, that might be because he's given no one the chance to get clingy. Before Jessica, his longest relationship was a one-night stand that ran into brunch.

How did I get here? He knows what attracts him to her. She dresses well, with a lacy white blouse and distressed denim that hugs her hips. But he did not know why she stays with him; it has nothing to do with his looks. Black hair, brown eyes, and smaller than average height weren't exactly cover model material. "Appearances are superficial," Jessica has told him. She likes his inquisitive nature and brilliant mind. That strokes his ego a bit. *Maybe that's why I've stayed with her this long,* Jack thinks. He gets lost in his thoughts and doesn't notice Jessica speaking until she tugs incessantly on his arm.

"Hey, earth to space case, anyone home?" She pretends to knock on his head. "Are you even listening?"

He stares into her sparkly hazel eyes. "No, I am. Uh—cheerleading... Go wildcats, woohoo."

Judging by the shifts in her expressions, she didn't appreciate his joke.

"I-I well... sorry," he stammers.

"Oh my God! You haven't heard a word I said, have you? Your body is here, but where's the rest of you? Buried in the clouds, I presume." Jessica let go of his arm, which she'd been squeezing so hard it had gone numb.

Jack clears his throat. "Sorry, I got distracted for a moment."

"Distracted by what? Is there another woman? Who is this bitch?" Jessica slams her fist into her hand, berating him with questions. She looks like she is preparing to go to war with a nonexistent woman.

He puts his hands on her shoulders. "Jessica, it's not another woman." He hesitates. "I would never cheat, my father cheated on my mom, and I will not become him," he says quickly, covering his mouth like he has just mentioned something he shouldn't have. His body tenses as his jaw clenches. He hopes nothing else will escape his mouth. He couldn't deal with the idea that someone might think of him as a cheater. He is many things, but not that. "I'm sorry. I was just enjoying my time with you. My mind got caught up in this moment," he says in hopes this will reassure Jessica enough. He isn't in the mood to argue right now.

"Aw, Jacky poo! I knew you cared about me." She smiles, clearly pleased with his response. "Also, this is the first time you have ever mentioned your father. You're finally opening up!"

"I'm an open book," Jack says, finding her changing moods frightening.

"No, you're a cat." She places a finger on his lips. "Sorry, I work at a shelter, so I spend a lot of time with animals. I put people into two categories: cats and dogs. I know it's weird, but you like me for my quirky personality. Having a dog differs from having a cat. Dogs are happy to be with people. They will sit there and wait for their owner to come home. Dog people are similar. They live for others. They are happy and open people and get their energy just being there for others. You probably know this, but cats aren't like that. They are distant, live to be waited on, and are only loyal to those they feel deserving. Cat people are closed off and fiercely independent."

Jack rubs the back of his head and grimaces. "So, is that a bad thing? Being a cat doesn't sound great."

"There is one thing that the cat person has over the dog. That is undying loyalty. In comparison, the dog person will share his bone with anyone who glances in his direction. The cat person won't open up to anyone unless they trust them completely. When a cat opens up to you, consider yourself lucky. That's why you're sharing yourself with me makes me the luckiest woman on this beach."

"Interesting," Jack says. Her theory makes sense, though he doesn't want to break the sad news that he would rather be a duck, because they have wings.

Jessica squeezes his arm again. "Jack, I love you!"

Her words terrify him. He stands paralyzed with the fear of breaking this girl's heart. *I can't be responsible for that.* He's seen firsthand what a heartbroken woman looks like and never wants to be the man who causes that.

After Jack drops off Jessica, he sneaks into his mother's house. She's normally asleep but if he rummages loud enough, she may wake. He knows it's rude, but he just left a girl who told him she loves him and if anybody knew what to do, it would be his mother. He knows she will help, but he didn't expect her to round the corner with a bat. She is disheveled, black hair in tangles as she comes down in her pajamas, brown eyes wide with fear.

"Ahh!" Molly screams, swinging her bat until she recognizes Jack and places her hand over her heart. "Jacky, I thought you were a burglar. You know you should text me before you come over!"

Jack smiles as he lowers the bat from his mother's hand. "I didn't want to interrupt your slumber. Lord knows you need your beauty sleep!" He turns away to rummage through the cupboards again.

Molly tightens her grip on the bat. She puts the bat down and slaps him across the head.

"Ow, Ma, child abuse!" Jack says, rubbing his head, turning around, and realizes his mother is red in the face.

"Please, you stopped being a child the moment you moved out. Speaking of, why are you here? Don't you have your own apartment you can ransack?"

Jack rubs the back of his head. "I would, but nothing beats a home-cooked meal." He smiles like a child, but his mother is scarily intuitive and glares at him. "Fine, I may have just done a terrible thing."

She takes her son's hand and leads him to the small dining room table. "What is it? Did you kill someone? You know, the only murder I will accept is your father's."

Jack shifts in his chair, tussling his hair. "No, I'm afraid it's worse!"

Molly fixes Jack's hair. "Boy, the only thing worse than murder is genocide and not talking to your mother. Since you are here now that leaves genocide, so when do we expect the police to come?"

"Actually, they're here now. I just told them to stay quiet so we could talk before I'm shipped off to Guantanamo."

"Boy, don't make me slap you again!"

Jack protects his head jokingly as he slumps down in his chair. "I think I broke a girl's heart!"

"Oh, that's it. You snuck into my house for that!" Molly puts her hand over her chest.

"And your home cooking!"

"Boy don't bullshit me. You're eating a peanut butter sandwich. I'm sure you can make that in your apartment. Now tell me what's bothering you."

Jack sits up, fiddling with his hair. "You know Jessica?"

"That loud redhead you brought over for dinner last Sunday. Yeah, I know of her."

"She told me she loved me."

"And you told her to drop dead and go to hell?"

Jack nods but stumbles. "No! Damn, Ma! What did she do to you?"

"You should know. I never liked redheads. Why can't you date a beautiful brunette like your mom?"

"Why would I want to date someone that looks like you?"

Molly reaches across the table and slaps Jack's head once more. "Anyway, back to the subject at hand. What did you really say?"

Jack rubs his head. "Let me see if I can remember with all the head trauma. I said nothing. I just took her home and stayed silent the whole way there."

"And why was this?"

"I don't know. She's a splendid girl, but things were moving too fast, and I didn't want to end up..."

"Like me," his mom finishes his thought fighting back the tears.

Jack knows he screwed up. His father left when he was a young boy. Even though he can barely recall his face, this has always been a sore subject with his mother. He looks at the worn Rolex on his wrist. *Maybe if I hadn't been wearing this.* Regardless, he wouldn't say it was her; it could never be her. She is the strongest woman he knew. He would be lucky to be half the man she wants him to be. This look of pain and grief is not what he wants to see. He grabs her hands and kisses them.

"No, Ma, I'd be lucky to end up like you." Jack pauses carefully, trying to craft his words. "If I just leave, I'm afraid I'll be like Dad."

"Oh, Jacky, you will never be like that man." Molly chuckles. "Unless you marry the girl, get her pregnant, fuck your secretary, and leave your family with not so much as a birthday card for your son."

Jack looks at the worn-out Rolex again. His mom's words made him think that maybe he never intended to receive the watch, but he needs to know what his next step will be. So, he asks, "What should I do, Ma? Just walk away or talk to this girl?"

"Obviously talk to her, you idiot!"

"Okay, Ma. What's wrong with me? Why can't I even say those three words ironically?"

Molly strokes her chin. "I have concluded..."

"Yes?" he asks with a mischievous smile.

"There is nothing wrong with you."

"Okay. So why couldn't I tell her?"

"Easy, she's not the one."

"Ma, you know I don't believe in that crap."

"Fine, she is not one of the women to whom you will say those three words."

"How will I know?"

"One day, you will meet someone that will take all your words away, and you will want nothing more than to make her smile. She'll make you do and say things you never thought you would. Instead of running away, you will embrace her when you find her."

Jack doesn't know what to say. He is quiet for a moment. "Did Dad make you feel that way?"

"Once, a million years ago," she says. "Don't let my past affect your future, Jacky. I know you're a smart boy, but you can be so stupid sometimes. Promise me that when you find someone who makes you feel something, you will open up your heart to her."

"I promise."

"Good, now get out of my house." She shoos him away with a smile.

"Ma, you know I love you, right?"

"I know. It's kind of a requirement since you're my son."

"Okay, bye, Ma."

"Love you too, Jacky! Bye!"

2

—.—

WORK AND PLAY

<u>One year Later</u>

Jack looks at the building with disdain. It's the same gray building he's visited hundreds of times. He has been doing this for over four years. The air inside is always cool, almost uncomfortably so. He has an appointment. The only thing that would motivate him to show up to his appointment is the fact that the streets smell like urine, and the smog makes everything worse, like he is in an oven. *Money and more pleasant smells,* he thinks as he holds his breath walking in the building.

Inside, he approaches the receptionist, a stunning young brunette with a piercing gaze that tears right through him.

"Is Dr. Ramos in?" Jack asks, trying to compose himself. He glances at the name plaque on her desk, which has "Cindy Rose" scribbled on it.

Cindy, he thinks. *What a beautiful name.*

She wears a blue floral dress cut to show a modest amount of cleavage accented by the gold music note necklace that sits perfectly below her neck.

"Dr. Ramos will see you in five minutes," she replies. A flush of pink colors her cheeks and she looks down nervously, arranging the papers on her desk.

Jack raises an eyebrow as if to ask a question.

"Is there anything else I can help you with?" she says, not looking up to meet his gaze.

"Yes, I have five minutes and I'd like to use it to get to know you," he says, leaning in.

Cindy chuckles. "You'll need more than five minutes for that."

Jack smiles excitedly. She is interested in talking. "I guess you're right. Let's start with a simple question: why do you work here, why not be a part-time model somewhere?"

"Are you saying I'm too pretty to work here?" she says, brushing her hair behind her ear.

"I never said that. You're putting words into my mouth, Ms. Cindy Rose."

"What's your name, salesman? Who wants to hear my life story?"

"Jack Salinger, the guy who has a two o'clock at your service." Jack looks down at his watch for effect. "I'm sorry, a 2:05 with Dr. Ramos. But I'd rather have an all-day o'clock with you."

"Do you use that line a lot?"

"Almost exclusively."

"Does it ever work?"

"Never."

The red light on her desk turns green, signaling Dr. Ramos is ready to see Jack.

"It's too bad," Cindy says with a shy smile. "I was enjoying our chat."

Jack pulls out his phone and hands it to her. "Add your number, please."

She doesn't hesitate and hands his phone back a few minutes later. "I guess I'm just going to have to get your life story over dinner!"

"You can get me dinner in five minutes?"

"I guess we can extend it to as long as it takes to get your story."

Cindy smiles. "Okay, it's a date!"

"Bye, for now, Cindy Rose."

"See you soon, Jack Salinger."

<u>Eight months later</u>

"Jack, wake up," Cindy murmurs in his ear.

Jack lazily stretches his body and opens his eyes, smiling at the beautiful girl in his bed. He leans over to kiss her good morning and then grabs his watch from the night-stand.

"Not this tired old gag," Cindy says, rolling her eyes.

"I thought you loved the watch gag?"

"I'm not in the mood for it this morning. Can you take me home?" Jack realizes she is already dressed and ready to leave.

"Sure, what's the deal?"

"There is no deal. I just want to go home!" She crosses her arms, glaring at Jack, who is still trying to process the morning.

"You're crabby this morning."

"What's that supposed to mean?" she says.

She's woken up in a terrible mood today.

"I'm sorry. Let's get some coffee and something to eat. That'll put us both in a better mood," Jack says hoping to avoid a conflict.

"No, take me home."

"Fine!" Jack says, finally getting out of bed to meet Cindy's unwavering glare.

They drive in silence that morning. Jack wonders why Cindy is on the defensive today. They have a solid rela-tionship; only fighting over minor things, such as who has the better taste in music or if one of them says something out of turn. Today feels different. Her body language and tone of voice mirrors that of someone who doesn't want to see him. Jack has seen this behavior in many clients before.

Cindy is not some client, he thinks. *Just give her space and she will come around.*

Later that evening, Cindy shows up back at his apartment to apologize.

"Hey, maybe the problem is we are spending too much time away from our apartments," Jack says, like he has solved the riddle she left him with this morning.

"What are you getting at, Salinger?"

"I'm saying we should move in together."

"I have one unpleasant morning and the solution is to move in together. You must be the smartest dumbass I know."

"It's just a suggestion."

"It's a crazy suggestion!" she says. "What will happen when I refuse to have sex with you? Are you going to tell me we should have a baby?"

"What? No! I thought since we've been together for eight months, the next logical step would be for us to move in together."

"Okay, you want to move to the next step. First, you need to tell me you love me!"

"What does that have to do with anything? That's not our problem."

"Bullshit it's not!"

"What are you saying, Cindy?"

She paces around the room nervously. "I was angry because I woke up this morning and realized that I have been waking up next to a man for the past eight months that has not once told me he loves me. Even though I've said it dozens of times, you can't even say it once. Why should I stay with you?"

"It's implied. I wouldn't be with you if I didn't feel that way about you. Plus, I didn't know you wanted me to say it."

"You didn't know?" she asks, throwing her arms in the air in exasperation.

"Why do you want me to say those words? Are my actions not good enough?"

"No, they're not! I know you're working on some family things, but that's not an excuse! Ever since I was a little girl, I have wanted two things. One was to marry a musician. The second was to have someone whisper three little words in my ear every night! Do you know what those three words are?"

"Go to sleep," Jack chuckles at his joke.

"This is no time to be funny, dickhead! Those words are something you seemed to have erased from your tiny brain. I love you!"

He knows she is right. He doesn't want her to be right so out of spite he yells, "Fine, I love you! I love you, Cindy Rose! Are you happy? Is that what you wanted?"

"Real classy, jackass!" she retorts and storms out of the apartment.

"Aww, where are you going?"

"I'm going to The Note. Don't follow me!" she yells before slamming the door behind her.

Jack stands there in defeat and mumbles to himself, "I hate that place, anyway. Bunch of hippies who can't decide whether they want to be a Mexican or Chinese restaurant."

<u>Four months later</u>

Ever since the fight about those three words, Cindy has been calmer, and they've had no disagreements. Tonight as they are walking in the park they are approached by a tall blond man who looks like a cover model to Jack.

The man stares at them for a moment until he embraces Cindy with familiarity. "Hey, Cindy. How are you?"

"Hi, not sure if we've met before," Jack says as he glances around at Cindy trying to gleam an answer.

The blond man looks at Jack and just smiles. "Oh, sorry man, I'm Mark. You may have heard of me. I'm the lead singer/guitarist of the band Sasquatch Sabotage. We're headliners at The Note where I met this little lady."

Jack looks at Cindy and notices how uncomfortable she seems. She keeps trying to make eye contact with Mark, which really unsettles him.

"Oh yeah, I've heard your stuff," he says. "Cindy plays your songs all the time. Not bad. I'd say if you get your stuff out there enough, you may pick up a real record deal."

"What is that supposed to mean?"

Mark puffs out his chest, squaring up to fight until Cindy gets between both men, leaving her hand on Mark's chest. "That's enough. You two save your piss for the urinals." She puts her hand down on Jack's side and rubs her hand down Mark's torso discreetly. "Jack didn't mean it that way. He knows you're talented, Mark."

Mark nods. "Okay, my bad."

Jack's not sure what to make of the situation, until he sees a glance between the two that he probably wasn't supposed to see. After some back and forth in his head he has a disturbing realization. "Oh my God! You two are fucking!"

Mark and Cindy share a glance before turning their heads to avoid any further form of eye contact. Jack waits for someone to tell him he is way off base, but nothing comes out of anyone's mouth as they just stare awkwardly at him.

Cindy's eyes water as she whimpers, "Jack."

Jack trembles, holding back what he could only describe as a public scene. "Don't you dare try to justify! Tell me I'm wrong and we can move on like normal people."

Cindy glances at Mark, then at Jack with tears more freely falling down her face. "I'm sorry Jack. But..."

"Thought so. You two enjoy your life of sin together!"

Jack walks away, fighting back tears. Cindy says something inaudible to Mark before chasing after Jack all the way to his apartment. He gestures for her to come in. She bows her head as she follows Jack in. Being in the confines of the apartment gives Jack the permission he needs to release his emotions. "How could you!" he screams, tears streaming down his face.

Cindy takes a deep breath in an attempt to stay calm. "I'm sorry, Jack, but it just happened!"

"Oh, so he just slipped on a banana peel and landed his dick into you!"

"Don't be so crass, Jack."

"You have no right to tell me how to act! How long has it been?"

Cindy grows quiet, mumbling under her breath. Jack clenches his fist, his whole body shaking in anger. "It's not a rhetorical question Cindy. How long have you two been fucking behind my back?"

Cindy whimpers. "Four months. I met him on the night of our fight."

Jack was trying to be rational, but his emotions were winning the battle against his logic. "You let me be a cuckold for four entire months!"

"Nobody uses cuckold anymore. Get with the times!"

"Don't change the subject! Why would you betray me? And make me look like an idiot for four months!"

Cindy took several labored breaths, repositioning herself so she could speak more properly. "I really am sorry, Jack. That fight wasn't just about you telling me you loved me. I realized I didn't mean it when I said it either. Sure, when we started dating it was great, but after a while I realized we were drifting apart. I stayed because you were trying so hard to keep us together. Then four months ago I saw Mark. He sparked something in me I never experienced with you; passion and excitement."

Jack paces, rubbing his temples, trying to make sense of the situation. "Why did you not break up with me first?"

"I didn't want to lose you."

"It's too late for that!"

"No, it's not that simple. You were sweet, but Mark has me the most excited I've ever been with anyone. I have no justifiable reason why I stayed with both of you. I just know I wanted both of you in my life."

Jack shakes his head. "Bullshit! Deep down there is only room in your heart for one of us and it's clear who that is."

Cindy tries to grab Jack's hand, but he rejects it. She begs, "Please, Jack, I never meant to hurt you!"

Jack grows silent. There's nothing she can say that would ease his pain. She made her choice, and he can barely stand the sight of her. "Get your things and get out!"

"Jack!"

"Out!"

Cindy obliges, but Jack doesn't look at her as she heads toward the door before turning around. "I hope we can still be friends."

Jack says nothing as she closes the door behind her and walks out of Jack's life.

3

DAMMIT

<u>Five months later</u>

Jack walks into an empty apartment. He stares at the door, his only way in and out. A choice he has to make every day. In or out. If he stays inside, he can hide in his solitude, misery, trapped in his mind until he cries himself to sleep. If he chooses outside, he can escape his pain and be distracted by worldly pleasures. The outside has women.

He chooses the outside.

During the next few months, he immerses himself at work, faking smiles, creating superficial relationships, putting in an unhealthy amount of overtime, and avoiding every pretty receptionist like a nasty disease. He hooks up with women he has no plans to get to know. Despite his attempts to escape his reality, he came to the sobering reality that he is still a human being, with that annoying flaw humans have of needing sleep, so begrudgingly he'd return to his place of misery. He sees the room that reminds him of the fight he had with Cindy five months ago. For almost half a year, he isn't happy. He knows this is unhealthy but refuses to give up his misery. He thinks how much easier it would be to move so he won't have to be reminded of Cindy ever again.

After a long day of work, Jack stumbles into his bed face-first, disgruntled and exhausted. He turns himself over, scrolling through his phone before plugging it in.

His eyes widen with a somber look, and he jumps to his feet. "No, are you fucking kidding me!" He throws his phone against the wall. "That's definitely broken now. Great job, Jack." He picks up his phone and the only thing he can see is a static image of an engagement ring.

"Dammit!" he screams.

Throwing the useless device against the wall again, he heads out to the distractions of the world hoping to quiet his thoughts with alcohol. He finds himself in an empty bar with neon signs where he and the bartender share a greeting of familiarity.

"The usual?" the husky bartender asks.

Jack nods. A few seconds later a glass of brown liquid appears in front of him. Jack swallows the drink, then stares at the empty glass for a moment. Jack puts the glass down gingerly, bowing his head and burying his face in his hands thinking about the last picture he saw on his phone. He quietly whimpers in a muffled cry, "Dammit." The image of Cindy and Mark engaged burns in his mind.

4

— • —

CONNOISSEUR

<u>Six months later</u>

Jack finds himself at a beach wedding he had no intention of going to. He tries to keep his composure as random people trickle in, locating their seats.

It's a perfect summer day to have a beach-side wedding. The temperature is perfect. The only sound to be heard beyond the chatter of several well-dressed people talking among friends is the crash of the ocean meeting the ground. The dark blue body of water is painted by the hue of the sunset slowly sinking out of sight. The sand is golden, with slight glimmers of light, undisturbed and perfect for miles down the beach. Jack continues to notice the small area where he's sitting. Just out of view of the bride, everything is decorated to perfection. Four white picket fences square off the little piece of land they occupy. Two of the fences are held together by a wicker arch, decorated in fully bloomed white roses. In the archway stands a white podium with the wedding officiant holding a bookmarked bible. Mark stands to his left with a childish grin on his face. He wears a three-piece gray suit with a white rose lapel, his hair in a man bun. Behind him stand two men: Brad, the drummer, and Chad, the bass player in his band. They are not as well-dressed, but they still match his gray suit and blue tie.

On the officiant's right stand three of Cindy's sisters; Kendra, Abby, and Stacy all differing in age but who are mirror images of Cindy. They each wear a knee-length navy blue dress in the same shade as the men's ties. They all stand on a white cloth, the same white color cloth as the runner that separates the white folding chairs arranged in two ten-by-ten rows. Every chair is occupied, except for one on the right side and one on the left.

Cindy tried to reach out to Jack months prior, but he wanted nothing to do with her. One day he received a save the date under his door. He regrets ever agreeing to this, but he thought sitting in a corner seat he could observe and not be noticed. But the crowd is so massive he doubts she would even recognize his presence.

Suddenly, the wedding march plays as a happy young blonde girl in a pink ruffled dress skips down the aisle, scattering red rose petals. Once she lands in front of the alter, her mother coaxes her over to sit down. Next all the guests stand up. Jack stays seated a moment longer before standing himself, knowing that the bride is coming down the aisle now. He looks over at Mark and sees his eyes widen with excitement. Begrudgingly, he turns to look at Cindy. She's beaming with that perfect bright smile that still makes his heart beat a little faster. Her hair is done up in a single braid that reaches to the small of her back, and on top of her head lays a headband with a thin veil draped over her perfect face. Her dress is a strapless, floor-length white gown. With each step toward the alter, you can see a glimpse of her shiny blue shoes. Around her neck she wears the gold necklace with the music note sitting right above her chest. She carries of bouquet of roses in her hands. She does not notice Jack. It's for the best.

The ceremony goes as it should; an exchange of rings, I do's, a few screaming children before the happy couple turned around to walk back down the aisle as husband and wife.

Jack sits at a table with total strangers. *Obviously, this is the extras' table,* he thinks. At least the bride's table is obscured from his view. "Does this wedding have an open bar or am I about to spend three paychecks buying alcohol?" he asks the man sitting to his right.

"Yeah, free drinks, bottomless champagne, catered dinners. This wedding has everything!" the guy chuckles. Clearly, this is the event of his year.

"Good to know, thank you." Jack flags down a server. His night is about to get much better.

"May I help you, sir? Would you like a plate of the chicken pate?"

"Yes, and I would like one of every drink on the menu, plus that bottomless champagne everyone is raving about."

"Are you sure, sir? That's over twenty-five different cocktails, ten types of wine and at least ten unique spirits. All watered down with just so much champagne."

"I'm positive. It's the only thing that will make this night palatable."

"Right away, sir." The server walks away, shaking his head in a chuckle, and returns a few minutes later with one other server to hand Jack his tray of drinks.

"You must be some kind of connoisseur," the man next to Jack says.

Jack smiles and takes a sip of one cocktail. "That I am my good sir, that I am."

After dinner is served, the couple have their first dance followed by the bouquet toss before it's time to cut the cake and start the many toasts of the evening. Cindy's sister, Kendra, stands up with tears in her eyes. She raises a glass of champagne in the air and says, "I would like to congratulate my sister on finding the love of her life..."

Jack sits at his table in the far corner drinking. Every time Kendra mentions things like the only man for Cindy or the wholesomeness of their union, Jack shudders. As the speech goes on, Kendra gets more emotional until there are more tears than words. Her speech becomes inaudible as she blubbers barely cohesive statements. She can barely whimper out her last sentence. "I love you sister and may Mark forever make you the happiest woman ever!"

This is the last straw for Jack. He stumbles to his feet, grabs his neighbor's spoon, and starts unrhythmically tapping his glass to draw everyone's attention. Once they all turn to him, he swallows the rest of his drink and in a slightly inebriated tone, he says, "I would like to compliment the 'happy' couple!" He looks at Cindy, hurt and disgusted. "Cindy, today you looked like a beautiful princess. And Mark," he turns his attention to the groom, "so did you!"

The crowd chuckles uncomfortably in response.

"Everything is beautiful, like a fairy tale threw up," he continues. "But you could have spent a little more on the food. I mean, you made this crappy beach look like something out of a Disney princess movie, it wouldn't have been such a stretch to get us some fish too."

The audience's chuckles slow down. Jack's expression changes as he turns his cheerful but condescending demeanor into a more serious and sad tone. "Many of you don't know this, but Cindy and I dated for over a year. But unbeknownst to me, several months into our relationship she started fucking this douche!" He points at Mark.

Mark stands up in an outrage, but Cindy stops him for reasons unclear to Jack; maybe she wants to hear him out.

Jack stumbles to the center, everyone standing in shock, but he pays no mind.

"For the last bit of our relationship, they were sneaking around behind my back. Some love story. 'My boyfriend was boring, so I spiced things up by sleeping with a dirty street musician'."

Cindy lowers her head. She is probably crying, but that doesn't deter Jack. Let her cry. He'd spent months doing the same. It's her turn now.

"I make a hundred thousand a year. He lives off tips and luck. So, tell me, princess, who loses in the long run? How did I lose you to him? I loved you, but that wasn't enough. You got 'your adventure.' You married your musician. What did I get? I got a promotion and moved to Salt Lake City with the Mormons. Okay, that's cool, more money to fill the hole you left in my life, I guess. But that's not fair. You still get to run home to the arms of this man," he points at Mark again, "who you ended up with dishonestly. You got a dream wedding with everything you ever wanted, built on a foundation of deception and sin. Meanwhile my honesty and loyalty gave me nothing that matters. I'm alone."

Jack bows his head, fighting back the tears forming in his eyes as he feels the heaviness of his face. The men at the bride's table stand up, ready to remove Jack. But he isn't at the wedding in his mind. He curls his hand into a fist.

"When I walk home, I'm alone. I drink alone. I eat alone. When I'm working, I'm alone. Every night, my head hits my pillow. I'm alone. Every waking moment of my life is nothing. And the worst part is that I'm a good person. I did nothing to deserve this loneliness. But you, a terrible person, you get everything you've ever wanted!" He takes a deep breath. "Mark, enjoy this bitch! You deserve each other!"

At that exact moment, Cindy's burly father and two other equally big gentlemen rush toward Jack.

"Alright, buddy, it's time to go!" her dad says.

"Also, I always thought that birthmark on your right ass cheek was stupid looking!" Jack yells as they drag him away.

The men cover his mouth and drag him far away from the reception.

"I never want to see your face again!" Cindy's dad threatens, shaking his fist in the air.

"It's a free country!" Jack says with a smug look on his face while still hoisted up by the two men.

Butch swings his right fist toward him and lands a blow on Jack's stomach. Jack spits out a splatter of blood, knocking the breath out of his lungs. The two men drop Jack as he falls. Cindy's dad stares down a helpless Jack with a look of pity before joining the other two men walking back into the reception. Jack stumbles to his feet. He tries to take a step, his legs give out, and he crashes to the ground face-first in the sand as he shuts his eyes, giving into his exhaustion and blacking out.

Jack wakes up the next morning to the wet tongue of a random golden retriever licking his face. Jack regains his composure and ends up face to face with this dog. The dog is pleased with himself. With a wet black nose and a coat of gold well-groomed fur, the gold tag hanging on his red collar reads Spike.

"Thanks, Spike," Jack mumbles. The dog lets out a single deep bark and runs toward a dark figure in the distance by the ocean.

5

SALT LAKE'S FINEST

<u>One month later</u>

Jack carries a suitcase in one hand and a messenger bag across his right shoulder.

"Yes, Mother. I know, Mother. No, I will not drink the punch," he says as he clenches the phone in his hand and contemplates smashing his phone just to end her barrage of questions. "A hotel. Yes, I will. Don't worry, the rest of my stuff is in Salt Lake already—I'll be fine. I'll call you when I land. Listen, I've got to go. My ride is here. Okay, love you, bye!"

He hangs up and gets into the cab. The driver turns back to Jack. "Where to?"

Jack drops his messenger bag to his side. "Airport."

As the car drives through the filthy city streets and mo-notone gray buildings, Jack realizes how little time he spent in downtown Los Angeles. He has spent ninety percent of his time in three buildings. Jack is excited to leave, not to get to his next destination but to leave his past behind. The past few years have only brought him sadness and confusion. To Jack, he's not saying goodbye to a city or his home. He's saying goodbye to women like Jessica and Cindy. He will not miss the lack of breathable air and the unpleasant smells of the city. If he never returns, he'll be fine.

At lift-off, the city slowly turns into mountains as he leaves behind everything to start a new adventure in Salt Lake City. It was a quick and uneventful flight.

As Jack goes to retrieve his luggage, he sees a short, portly man with slick black hair holding a cardboard sign with his name on it. He walks toward the man. "That's me," Jack says, extending his hand toward the man.

"Why hello, Mr. Salinger, welcome to Salt Lake." He shakes Jack's hand. "You're going to be working for Pharm-Tech's most heavenly branch, or at least that's what they say. I mean, we can talk about work on the car ride over there. Maybe we can stop for food."

Before Jack can respond, the man continues, "No, that will not work. Mr. Johnson said to bring you straight to the office. He wants to meet you right away." Tim stands back as he acts out a play. "I told him maybe he should let you rest. Flying is hard. But he said, 'Don't be ridiculous. He's Los Angeles's top salesperson.'" Tim wipes his brow as he stands tall to play Mr. Johnson's part. "'We need to bring him in right away. That's how business works.'" Tim changes his composure back to normal.

"I've been in the company for four years. I know how business works. Well, I guess since you're my new boss, I guess you get less work, but a monkey with a briefcase can work in sales. Who am I kidding? I'd buy anything from a monkey with a briefcase!" He laughs to himself.

"Oh, wait, I forgot to introduce myself. I'm Tim, Timothy Smith, but you can call me Tim. I'm your new ass-partner!" Tim says as he shakes Jacks hand more excitedly.

Jack finally frees his hand from Tim's grip with a look of fear. "Ass-partner?" he asks, opening his mouth to find the most diplomatic thing to say.

"Not ass-partner. I'm not gay. Not that there's anything wrong with being gay. I just like women a lot." Tim says this like he suddenly realizes his absurdity. Jack holds up his hand to stop him as he realizes he is backpedaling. "I mean, you're our new head of sales and I'm your assistant partner because I'm too experienced to be an assistant, but I do not have enough leadership experience to be a full partner. Look out because I'm eyeballing your job. I mean, I look forward to working closely with you. Not ass close but work close. We'll be like Lewis and Clark or Sherlock and Watson. I like that better. Did I mention I'm the top sales rep of the branch?"

Jack is taken aback. Sure, this man loves to talk, but he could not imagine how he's a salesperson, let alone a top performer. *Can he be the reason the branch is dying?* Jack quickly redacts those thoughts and watches as Tim spouts out more exposition until he turns around, beckoning Jack.

"All right, let's go Watson, we've already stood around here talking too much!" He grabs Jack's suitcase and starts walking.

Maybe I should have said nothing, Jack thinks.

During the car ride to the office, Jack tries to familiarize himself with his new city right away. It's different from Los Angeles which is big and spread out for miles while Salt Lake is small, compact, and surrounded by snow-covered mountains that look like they barricade the city. Tim talks Jack's ear off about women and work details that Jack has already been acquainted with.

They arrive at the Pharm-Tech building, which is remarkably like the one in Los Angeles except it is more compact and homier.

"Hey Debs!" Tim greets the receptionist as they exit the elevator. Her name sign actually says Deborah; judging by the scowl on her face, she isn't too fond of Tim's nickname. "Tell Mr. Johnson that the eagle has landed, and he has delivered the goods." He looks at Jack to get a reaction, but Jack is only half paying attention. The architecture distracts Jack already.

"Nobody is going to call you eagle, Timothy!" she hisses. He looks down in disappointment as she pushes a button on her phone. "Mr. Johnson, Timothy is here, with the new head of sales."

A silky, confident voice responds from the phone. "Great! Send them in."

"All right, you heard the man. Get out of my face!"

"All righty then, love you, Debs!" Tim blows her a kiss.

Deborah shoos him toward the elevator, and Jack silently follows. Guy Johnson has the corner office on the top floor.

Tim straightens his tie and his posture as he opens Mr. Johnson's door, letting Jack enter first as he follows, keeping a reasonable distance behind Jack.

Johnson's office is spotless and spacious, with not even a pen out of place. Tim clears his throat as he steps forward a bit. "Mr. Johnson, this is Jack Salinger."

Tim steps to the side, allowing Jack to meet eyes with the six-foot dapper man, who reaches out his hand to shake Jack's firmly. "Jackson Salinger, I've heard wonderful things about you. You better not disappoint me."

"It's just Jack, sir, a common mistake, but I won't hold it against you." Jack retracts his hand with a smug smile.

Mr. Johnson stands stoically for a moment, then suddenly leans his head back and bursts out laughing. "You'll fit in nicely here, Jack. Timothy, you can learn a thing or two from Jack here. He's got a pair on him!"

Tim promptly glares at Jack, who just notices a frightened glare piercing the back of his head.

The rest of the day goes by in a blur with basic logistics, how-to-dos, fake smiles, and repetitive training. Tim and Jack walk out and stand outside of the office. Tim turns to Jack and inquires. "So, where are you staying?"

"A hotel down the street until I can find a place downtown."

Tim stares at Jack in absolute shock. "No, you're not," Tim says with a smile, as if he knows something he didn't.

"What do you mean? In my briefing, it says I'm staying at the Hyatt?"

Tim smugly replies, "I talked to Mr. Johnson. He said you could stay with me. I have a guest room. And who knows? If I like you, maybe you can move in with me."

Jack thinks, *How can this man be so trusting*? He seems odd, but there is an optimism to him he hadn't seen in anyone he ever met. Maybe that is why he's a top performer. "What makes you so sure you can trust me?"

Tim smiles. "Honestly, I don't know if I can. You're a bit of a jerk, but like in most buddy cop movies, I can change you."

Jack laughs. This man is refreshingly honest. "Okay, your funeral."

Tim laughs. "Louis, I think this is the beginning of a beautiful friendship."

Jack shakes his head. "Casablanca. What are you, fifty?"

Tim bumps his shoulder. "Get used to it, I can quote movies all day."

Tim's apartment is clean and spacious. It has an open kitchen with gigantic windows, two bedrooms, and modest furniture. Unlike Jack's last place, it feels warm and lived in. Jack lived in isolation for so long he forgot what it felt like living with another person. Tim leads Jack around the apartment.

"Welcome to my humble abode, casa de Tim or casa de Tim y Jack now," Tim announces happily. "My room's on the left. Yours is on the right. I have a guest room for my family to come. I'm the youngest of five, so for a while it was a rotating door of people, but now it's just an empty bed and dresser." Jack looks at Tim with worry. "Don't worry, it's clean." Tim shows him where everything is located. "I hope you're clean because I enjoy keeping things tidy. But you look clean, so I hope my intuition is right about you, which it normally is. So, let's talk about ground rules. Keep your stuff clean and the main room clean. Your room is your own, so I don't care about that. When there's a sock on my door, don't come in because," he winks, "it means I have company, so when the bedroom's a rocking, don't come a knocking. Anyway, those are my only rules. Questions?"

"Yeah, got it. The rocking and knocking means sex. I didn't peg you for such a lady killer." He winks at Tim, nudging him. "You get 'em, tiger."

"Not to brag, but I've been with almost a handful of women!" he says, holding up three fingers proudly. "So, yea, I'm a stud, but don't worry, young virgin, one day you can catch up to me. So, what's your—you know women or men, whatever you're into, this is a judgement-free zone. I mean, well, let's just say how many people have you slept with?"

Tim stares intently at Jack, who starts toward the open door he assumes is his. As he walks away, he turns to Tim. "Over three, my chaste warrior."

"Four?" Tim says, worried.

Jack shakes his head.

"Ten!" Tim says in disbelief.

Jack shakes his head.

"Twelve?" Tim says in utter awe.

Jack looks around the empty room, nods and turns to Tim and in a sarcastic seductive voice, he mocks, "Good night, stud!"

"Okay, fine, don't tell me," Tim says. "Just lift one hand in the air if it is over twenty."

Jack smiles and slowly lifts his hand in the air. He enters his new bedroom and shuts the door behind him.

6

▬ ▪ ▬

FINALLY

<u>One week later</u>

Jack has got Salt Lake figured out to a tee. With a mix of high curiosity, research, and the grid system, Jack quickly figured out what he needs. By week two, he had moved in. The process for getting Tim's approval was easy, considering how trusting he is. Jack found a favorite coffee place, bar, meditation area, running paths, and knew how to contact most of his clients.

On a Wednesday, three weeks after Jack made the move to Salt Lake, he's standing on a bridge in a quaint park he discovered while getting to know the city. Jack is standing listening to music as he watches two white and green ducks playing in the water. As Jack sits watching the show, his phone goes off.

"What's up?" On the other side of the phone, Tim rattles on endlessly.

Jack wonders if he'll ever be able to get a word in when he finally does. It's only two words at a time. "Calm down, Tim, it's just a roof. I'll meet you up there in ten. Okay, bye, see you then."

Tim's apartment complex is new. The rooftop was closed for a while, but today's the day it is finally opening up. As Jack reaches Tim, he takes in the roof's sight. It's a beautiful patio roof top with lights that glow yellow on the warm summer night. The ground is a red brick lain with white cement. It has a gazebo in the corner with some lawn chairs and fake grass in another corner. In another is a gated hot tub covered with a sleek blue cover. The rest is a huge open area, the edge with a step-down area shield with a black guard rail that has an outlook containing a breathtaking view of the city with snowcap mountains for a backdrop.

Tim did not notice Jack approaching him because, like him, he's been caught up in the sights also, but his eyes are fixed in one place.

"So, buddy, what do you think? Was it worth the wait?" Jack asks with a playful gesture. He braces himself for a monologue response, but shockingly, Tim stays silent. "Hello?" He waves his hand in front of Tim's face. "Earth to space case, you are never quiet. What magic spell has struck my chatty bard silent?"

Wordlessly, Tim raises his finger and points to a girl sitting with her back facing them, drawing.

"Oh, I see." Jack smiles. "Well then, let's go talk to her."

That snaps Tim out of his daze. "Yes, that was exactly what I was thinking," he responds. "Oh, and by the way, dibs."

"Okay, tiger, but first you have to talk to her and not stand there like an idiot." Jack chuckles as they walk toward the girl.

The girl looks back to see the two approaching, then stands. She isn't especially tall but stands straight with her head tilting up to raise her tiny nose to the sky. She brushes her bright blonde hair out of her face. She straightens her light green cardigan and dusts off her white jeans, preparing herself for a confrontation. Jack does not blame her; after all the two strange men who were bigger than her had just approached. This would be intimidating no matter the situation. She is standing as tall as she can, but she still does not match the height of Tim or Jack. Her face has an appropriate amount of makeup so as to not obscure her natural beauty. Jack glances at the pillow she was sitting on. The red pillow that she places her worn sketch pad and a well-chewed pencil on. She had been drawing the view.

"Come here often?" Tim asks.

"Considering the fact that this is the first day it's been open, no," she responds, without even looking at him.

Tim stands silent a moment. Maybe he realizes how dumb that question made him look. She gazes directly into the eyes of the two men. The moment she meets Jack's eyes, he is instantly drawn to her bright, artic blue eyes that remind him of paintings of beautiful glaciers and the soft pink lips that perch as she looks like she was studying the situation thoroughly.

"I'm sorry, let me start over," Tim says. "Hi, I'm Tim. This is my friend, Jack. I thought you were cute, so I just had to come over."

She pays little attention to his spiel because she can't stop staring at Jack but to acknowledge the nervous Tim's inquiry, she plays along.

"Hi Tim, I'm Sarah!"

7

─ ◆ ─

I AM AN ARTIST.

<u>Four years earlier</u>

Sarah sits across from an older woman wearing rectangular glasses. Sarah's hands are on her knees gripping her dress. As she feels a drop of sweat drip down her forehead, she then licks the salty droplet off her lips as she tries to calm her shaking. The air is chilly, but she is warm. The woman's stare is intense, not helping Sarah's uneasiness. The woman examines a painting Sarah painted with thorough eyes.

Nodding, the woman relays, "Um-hm... Yes, I see... interesting." She takes off her glasses. "Well, I will say this: you have a vast potential, your grades are impressive, and your test scores are more than perfect. This is an art school; although academic prowess is important, the most important aspect must be your art. Tell me, Miss Reeding, why should we consider you?"

Sarah shifts in her chair as she answers with a smile, "Mrs. Harding, I've wanted to be an artist for as long as I can remember. I see the beauty in everything. My parents always told me to follow my dreams. Not only did I want to come here to show my parents that I can follow my heart, but this also would be a lifelong dream of mine."

Mrs. Harding sits up, staring at Sarah with no emotion. "Would you say you're here for your family or yourself?"

"Myself!" Sarah says, raising her voice.

Mrs. Harding stands up with her hands behind her back. "Ms. Reeding, we get thousands of applicants in an academic year. And I review hundreds of paintings by hundreds of artists that have the same hopes and dreams as yourself. So, I will ask you again, why should we accept you?"

Sarah jumps up. "With all due respect, Mrs. Harding, because if you don't accept me, it would be the biggest mistake of your life!"

Mrs. Harding slams the desk, leaning toward Sarah. "I hear that exact statement ten times a day. And only one percent of the time can an artist back up their words. And frankly, Miss Reeding, your art is not backing up your words." She picks up the painting, showing it to Sarah. "When I look at this painting, I see a tree, a beautifully rendered tree, with excellent detail. But you know what I don't see? The artist who drew this tree."

Sarah thinks of all the hours and labor she put into this piece, trying to piece together what Mrs. Harding's trying to say. "I don't understand. I painted that."

Mrs. Harding stands straighter, adjusting herself. "What I'm saying is this piece has no identity. Yes, I know you painted it. Anyone can paint a picture, but few can paint a piece with an identity. When someone observes one of your pieces, they should understand its story. Each piece should have its own unique identity. Ninety percent of people who buy art don't buy pieces just because they look pretty. They buy pieces because it makes them feel something. The other ten percent end up in lobbies of businesses and hotels as decorations." She sits down, prompting Sarah to do the same. "I don't see it in your work. I'm sorry, but we can't accept you this semester. But know this is not to discourage, but to encourage you. There is always next year. My advice is next time you apply, submit multiple pieces--ten pieces—at minimum. It will increase your chances. I like you, but I think your skills need to be refined. Do you have a plan B?"

Sarah clenches her fist in her lap. "My sister recommended a beauty school, but like a pregnancy, my plan A is not to get to plan B."

Mrs. Harding smiles at Sarah. "Focus on living your life however you feel necessary but try not to let this impede on your life." Mrs. Harding stands up and shakes Sarah's hand. "I truly hope we can meet again."

Sarah nods. "Thanks for everything, Mrs. Harding."

Sarah leaves the campus, meeting her sister outside by her car with a big grin. "How'd it go?" Sarah weeps uncontrollably as Ruth embraces her, rocking her little sister back and forth in a comforting, yet sarcastic tone. She iterates, "That good, huh?"

Sarah, still crying, slaps Ruth's back. "Ruthie, that's not funny!"

Ruth lets go and grabs Sarah by the shoulder. "Sarah, look at me." Sarah, whimpering, looks up at Ruth with wide eyes. Ruth just smiles and slaps her face gently. "This isn't the end of the world. Now let's get ice cream. We're in San Francisco. It'd be a crime to visit without going to Ghirardelli."

Sarah rubs her face as Ruth runs to the driver's side. "Okay, but you didn't need to slap me."

Sarah ends up going to the American Beauty Academy in the west valley where she met Julie and Cliff.

Julie is bold, with a curvy figure, giant red hair, hazel eyes, and a loud personality. Cliff is a tall lanky brunette with visibly green eyes. He had a wardrobe as colorful as his personality. Instantly, they all knew this was going to be a great friendship.

_ℓℓ_

<u>Two years later</u>

Sarah paces back and forth. Each step makes the floor squeak. Her frantic rambling is disturbing.

Julie jumps in front of Sarah, trying to stop her from pacing around. "Calm down! You're going to put a hole in the floor with all that pacing."

"Frankly, it would be an improvement. The only color we have in this place is Sarah's drab painting of that tree," Cliff chimes in.

"Fuck you, Cliff," Sarah snaps. She's tired of Cliff's stupid comments about her work. He knows nothing about art, anyway.

"Damn, I'm sorry, it's a good painting. We don't need two Julies in the apartment!"

"Get fucked, Cliff!" Julie barks.

"Whoa, I'll leave." Cliff puts his hands up as if signaling surrender. "You two need to warn me when you join a bitch cult."

Julie approaches him slowly. "Oh, please, if there were any kind of bitch cult, you'd be queen!"

Cliff snaps back, "I will happily be queen of anything! If it means reigning over you."

Julie drives her finger into his chest. "Boy, I will slap you straight!"

"You wouldn't dare!"

Sarah realizes in her panic that she started this argument. Cliff is annoying but he didn't deserve the verbal lashing Julie is unleashing on him. She did what she always did to break the tension even though she had no idea why she did it. In a valley girl accent, she said, "Like, oh my god, you guys! This is like too much!"

It has the effect she is hoping for. Cliff and Julie turn toward her and start laughing.

"You're right, we have nothing to fight about," Julie says. "I know you're nervous, but it's my mom. She's always wanted to start a business. she'll call." Julie embraces Sarah. "Besides, if my mom says no to our pitch to open up a salon, we'll just murder three people, so they have no choice but to hire all three of us." Sarah looks up to Julie, pursing her lips, but Julie just grins menacingly. "I'm kidding, we'll only break their hands."

Sarah breathes, calming herself. "Okay. It's just it's all of us or none of us. This is our last chance. If we don't open our own salon, we all will be separated." Sarah backs away from Julie. "Let's hope Julie's mom says yes, so we can spare those three innocent people's hands."

"You know the witch will probably end up maiming someone, anyway," Cliff says as he sticks his tongue out at Julie, who just flips him off. He then embraces Sarah. "Honey, you know nothing can tear us apart." Julie's phone rings and Cliff lets go of Sarah as they all huddle around Julie's phone she put on speaker.

From the phone, a voice comes booming out, "Baby, of course I'll invest in this salon! Only if you agree on calling it Big Mama's after yours truly!"

Julie jumps up in excitement. "Of course, Mama, I'd call it Mama's cooch if it made you happy!"

"Watch your mouth, young lady!" the voice claps back. "But I look forward to doing business with you kids. Bye now, kisses!"

"Kisses, Ma." Julie blows a kiss in response. "Guys, we did it!"

All three jump for joy.

8

—·—

HE'S PERFECT, RIGHT?

<u>A few months later,</u>

Sarah is reading a book at one of her favorite hole-in-the-wall coffee shops. A tall man with perfect features walks in, taking note of the sea of people nose-deep in their phones and laptops. She glances over her book and notices the barista swoon as he brushes his long fingers through his feathery black hair and bats his sapphire blue eyes at the young woman, making her melt. *Oh, he's one of those.* She grimaces. He orders his drink and walks up to Sarah, who quickly stops gawking and buries herself in her book.

"You know, if you're not careful, you will wind up labeled as the weird girl reading a book. That's not normal and we don't want that. That is saying something, seeing that there is a guy in the corner wearing a cat sweater in the summer," the blue-eyed man says, placing his hand on her table.

Sarah continues reading her book, pretending she hasn't heard a word he's saying. To get her attention, the man puts his hand on her book and lowers it until their eyes meet. An annoyed Sarah removes an earbud as the man smiles and waves with his other hand.

"His name is Fred!" Sarah lifts her book up and continues reading, with one earbud still in.

"Who?" the man asks curiously.

Sarah bookmarks her page and points to the man in the cat sweater. "The man you roasted in your sad attempt to pick me up. He comes in every day sporting a new sweater that his mom made for him to show off her amazing craftsmanship. After he finishes his cookies and coffee, he will go home happy to have made friends for the day. Especially when he meets you. His new friend with an expensive watch and a poor sense of people skills. Never knowing his new friend is a raving asshole! But Fred is pure, he is simple, he is happy. Three things jerks who put people down for their own gain will never be."

The man looks surprised by her words. He turns to look at Fred just as he finishes his drink and starts his rounds. The people who were nose-deep in their phones look up for a moment to smile at Fred, who doesn't have a care in the world. When he gets to their table, he waves at Sarah.

"Hi, Saraww, look at my shirt. It's got a kitty! Who's your friend?"

Sarah smiles at Fred, then points at the man and introduces him.

"You see, Fred, this is one of my business friends. His name is Mr. Poopy Pants!"

Fred grins. "Ha, Poopy Pants, that's a funny name!"

Sarah smiles and glances to see how the man would react to the obvious test she has just given him. The man smiles at Fred and reaches out his hand to him. "Actually, it's Dr. Poopy Pants."

"Okay, bye Saraww, bye Dr. Poopy Pants!" Fred says. He waves goodbye and exits the coffee shop.

The doctor looks at an amused Sarah. She never expected this reaction from him. He just shakes his head. "Really, Poopy Pants? What are you? Five? It's a good thing you're pretty, or I would walk off having made a thorough ass of myself!"

Sarah twirls her hair, and in a mocking tone, says, "Oh, you think I'm pretty?" She's tired of this statement said by men who have nothing better to compliment. The doctor looks distraught. In her mind, a weak-minded man would stay and defend himself or run off cowering with his tail between his legs. She hopes he will recognize her flirting. She waits.

"Okay, I guess I'll go!" the doctor says as he stands up.

Sarah knows she has to stop, but she wants to see how far she can take it. "Okay, bye, nice to meet you, Dr. Poopy Pants."

The doctor places his hands on the table and leans toward Sarah. "Okay, I don't understand why you are unphased by me. I'm a doctor, normally girls throw themselves at me after I pass their shit test, but you are unreactive. I know you're not stupid because stupid people don't read sports novels like Smash Ball. The author uses a ton of complicated words and weaves a story that is a lot to follow, but you call me elementary-style nicknames like Poopy Pants. So, tell me lady, are you gay, or are you taken because those are the only two options. Tell me which one it is so I can walk out of here with some shred of dignity."

Sarah smiles, standing to be on equal footing with the towering man.

"First off, just because you passed one shit test doesn't mean I'm automatically yours. So don't think just because you are some freakish male model doctor I am automatically attracted to you!" Sarah puts up two fingers. "Second, Smash Ball is a romance novel, not a sports novel. Anyone who reads books would know that, and last, did you ever think of a third option that I am just not interested in self-centered, egotistical bastards!"

The doctor and Sarah step to the side of the table where there is nothing between them. Sarah has a shift of perspective standing in the presence of this man and could not help but to admire him as much as she tries to resist. She's drawn to him. He not only looks perfect, but his smell is intoxicating. He grabs Sarah by the hips, moving them close together. The doctor smiles. "You finished your coffee a while ago. You could have left, but you stayed because you like me!"

The doctor brings his head so close to Sarah's they were one syllable away from kissing, Sarah, realizing what the man is trying to do, turns her head and responds smugly, "I was here first. Who says I should go!"

The doctor chuckles as he re-introduces himself into the gap Sarah creates. He pulls a card out of his briefcase, scribbles something on the back, puts it down, and grabs his possessions. Sarah glances at the card on the table, the front reads, "Dr. Jim Jones MD." and has his office number, and on the back is his cell number.

Jim and Sarah date for two years establishing themselves as a Bonafede power couple, with her being on his side in the many philanthropic events. Jim even invests in Big Mama's salon. They were a perfect couple until the night of their two-year anniversary. Jim went all out like he normally did with dinner at an expensive restaurant with valet parking, formal wear, and a bouquet of flowers. The two of them sit down at their usual table, sharing a glass of champagne. Sarah bites her lips as she clenches her dress with her fist because she knows tonight is the night she is going to break up with Jim.

"Hey, my father was crying on the phone today. Do you have any idea what that was all about?" she inquires, seeing what Jim could have told her father to make him that upset.

Jim looks up at the sky. "Nope, no idea."

Sarah looks at Jim curiously. "Okay."

The two situate themselves. Jim orders a bottle of champagne. Sarah is quite distraught because she is not sure how she's going to start the conversation. Luckily, it seems like Jim could read her face.

"Hey, Sarah, what's wrong?"

"I had a dream last night!"

"Okay, Miss Martin, what does that have to do with anything?" he says chuckling at his joke.

Sarah places her hands on her knees, clenching them into fists. "I know what it sounds like, but this was the most vivid dream I've had in a long time. I want you to know that it wasn't the dream that made me make this final decision. In this dream, we were both eating in a restaurant like this one. We were sitting right across from each other like we are now. You become smaller and smaller, and that is when I realize you are not getting smaller, but I am moving farther and farther away. Eventually you have disappeared into nothing. It is just me alone in complete darkness. You are gone and I am just there alone." Sarah tears up while Jim wipes the tears from her cheek.

"I do not understand. It seems like you just had a bad dream, what's that have to do with how you are feeling?"

"We need to break up!"

Both sit there looking at each other in a silence that seems like an eternity until Jim breaks the silence, sounding distraught himself. "I'm sorry. You've had one bad dream, and you want to throw away two years of love?"

Sarah catches her breath and tries to hold back more tears. "No, it's not the fucking dream! It is what the dream represents. It is something that has been weighing on my heart for months now. The dream was just the final push I needed to realize the true reason we will never work."

"I will never leave you or let you be alone, Sarah!"

"Dammit, just listen!" Jim sits back as Sarah gathers herself. "It's not the dream, it's what it represents. I'm holding you back and you know it. We met in a coffee shop two years ago. I was only thinking you wanted me for one night of sex and you'd be done, but it was more than that. I even thought I was in love, but then we started doing all these charity events. At first, I thought that was it, but then we did more, and these expectations were established, and people expect me to be this perfect piece of arm candy. There she is, Sarah, the doctor's girlfriend. Some days I think to myself, is that all I will ever be? The doctor's girlfriend whose only advancement in life is the doctor's fiancé, then the doctor's wife! But that's the thing, that is not who I am!"

Jim wipes a tear from her trembling cheek. "I never expected you to do anything. We can stop going to charity events if that makes you happy. I love you!"

"And I love you, but you and I both know that is not you. You are this perfect guy, and I am just the unsatisfied blonde on your arm pretending to be what I am not."

"You are the best thing that's ever happened to me." Jim pulls out a ring box from his pocket.

"D-don't, I can't let you throw away your potential for me. It's not just for your betterment, I need to find out who I am!" Sarah stands up, kisses Jim on the cheek and walks out the door, not turning back, especially not to show him the tears flowing down her cheek.

9

— · —

ODD FELLOWS

Back to the present

Sarah is surprised. Strange men have approached her before, but this duo seems different. She notices the two are in professional attire, like they both work at some kind of office. The one to approach her first, Tim, is very polished. He wore a tie with a crisp white shirt tucked in like he's really trying. His slicked back hair maybe shows he's trying too hard. The two could be brothers with their similar hair color and height. But the silent one is slightly darker, like he has some ethnic background. Also, unlike Tim, his blue work shirt is untucked with the sleeves rolled up like he cares about style, but he also does not conform with dress code. Maybe he just undid his tie and loosened up after work. Even though his wardrobe is clean and well-tailored, his hair's disheveled like he's in a constant state of worry. She thinks she might as well have fun with these two. It only made sense to her considering they are interrupting her during the best lighting of the day. In her mind, she has a strategy to break the loud one, and his frightened friend will either step in to defend him or go running. Either way, she will be free. Even though this pair seems odd, she could not help but be drawn to the silent one. His dark brown eyes are distant but have an intensity to them like he's concentrating on something. What it is baffles Sarah. It couldn't have been her because they do not follow her as she moves about.

"Hi Tim, I'm Sarah!" She starts playfully talking to Tim but looking at Jack.

Jack stands dumbfounded. Sarah notices he never made eye contact. Tim finally gains confidence and delivers a line. "Wow, you are the second most beautiful thing on this roof!"

Tim is proud of himself as Sarah, catching on to his cheesiness, retorts quickly and playfully. "Oh, really? What's the first?"

"Well, that would be me, of course, but don't worry, babe, you will catch up with a little work."

Sarah chuckles and looks at Jack, who looks like he is trying to solve a complex mathematical equation, paying no attention to what is going on in the moment. Sarah then turns to the confident Tim, and sees if she can break him.

"Okay, number four, what makes you think you're the most beautiful thing on this roof?"

"Well-I—wait, why did you call me number four?"

Sarah grins, knowing she struck something. "Because you are only the fourth most beautiful thing on this roof."

"Who are one through three?"

Sarah glances at the dumbfounded Jack, then back at Tim. "First is this incredible view, second is me, of course, and third is this handsome monk at your side." She gets closer to Tim and whispers in his ear, in a flirtatious manner, "Rendering you, Tim, number four, my sweetheart."

Tim gets visibly flustered and tries to defend himself, "Who? Jack? He is not even in this conversation so he doesn't even count!"

Sarah turns to look at the paralyzed Jack and rubs her finger down his chest. "Jack, is it? Where do I fall on your scale of beauty?" she asks, using the moment to further test Tim. This man has been harder to shake than she thought, but she stays because the longer Jack remains silent, the more she wants him to talk. Seeing if she can rattle him.

Jack robotically holds up three fingers.

Sarah steps back, placing her hands on her hips in defeat and a bit of shock. "Okay, my mute friend, who's number one?" She expects he will say himself or defend Tim, but Jack simply points to the breathtaking view. "Okay, who or what is number two?" she asks again, not expecting any audible answer at this point.

Jack is motionless, still not able to find words. After a moment of awkward silence, Sarah gives up and turns her attention back to Tim, who also looks at Jack with a bit of confusion. "So, Tim, what do you do for work?"

"Art!" Jack screams out in a sudden burst of excitement, and automatically loosens up like he has just been rebooted.

"Oh, he can speak," she says. "Or maybe he only knows one word and just remembered what it was."

But Jack is now a totally different person and continues the conversation like nothing happened. "You asked what I thought was number two. It is your drawing. I only saw a glance, but it captured the beauty expertly. So, if the view is number one, logical order dictates that a mirror image would be two, and you are only number three objectively. I would never put myself in front of a woman, and you beat Tim by a landslide."

"So, do you know art? Or are you just kissing up to me because I'm pretty?"

"I know enough."

"Okay, Mr. Knows Enough, what do you know?" she asks, hoping to pry deeper. "You just learned how to talk, don't stop now."

"I know you're an artist. Why would the first thing you do is draw when they just open up a new place? So complimenting your appearance only feeds your vanity more, but complimenting your work strikes a chord of pride. It's good, an artist always puts their work before themselves. It's what makes them unbearable. I know you have been playing my poor friend Tim, who compliments you as only a horny man knows. You have been playing silly games and giving us nothing to see if we would fold. Once Tim folded, you turned to me."

"I liked it better when you were silent. Okay, Mr. Know-It-All, what makes you so sure you're right about me?"

"I know people. I studied people in college. I work in a field that I thrive in for knowing people. You are an artist. There are only two types of artists, those that are famous and those that aren't."

"Have you always been this egotistical?"

Jack is a bit puzzled. "If by egotistical, you mean know I am right, yes. You don't get to the top by being stupid."

Sarah is thinking she now has Jack on the ropes. "What does making it to the top mean to you? How do you know when you made it in life?"

"Easy," Jack responds confidently. "It is to meet the max potential in your chosen profession, to make enough money to be comfortable for life, to be the best in your chosen career, where no one else can match you. Once you leave that legacy, you can die happy. In layman's terms you get to the top in life by getting to the top in your work. You're born, you work for sixty-five years, you retire, and you die."

Sarah shakes her head bemused and gives him a look of pity. "Life is more than just work. If you live just to work, then you live a miserable life. Success is certainly more than getting high marks at a job, because news flash, half of us work jobs we hate for money, which cannot buy you happiness."

"So, when do you know you've succeeded in life, then?" Jack says.

"When you're happy. Success is based on your measure of happiness. If you are satisfied with the life you lived, that is how you know you're successful. You don't work to live; you work so you can live. Life works for you when you let it."

Jack stands there silently for a moment before laughing. "Happiness is a fool's dream! Illusions of grandeur are put into our brains by stars on the silver screen, or by an author in a book. We live, we work, and we die. Period. There is nothing waiting for us in the end. We die expecting the cold and darkness of an empty grave. So all we have is the chance to make the most of what we can do right now so our families can survive while we rot in our graves. People break your heart, so get rid of them. The only true comfort you have in life is a glass of whiskey after a long day of work. That's the only thing I look forward to, because happiness is an illusion: but money is real. Alcohol is real. Food and a roof over our heads; all these things are real. If you can survive, that's all you will ever need. Happiness is just a crutch people latch on to, because they are too stupid to understand the reality of life!" Jack walks away, leaving both Tim and Sarah dumbfounded.

"What's his deal?" Sarah asks Tim.

"Something about getting drunk at a wedding, punched in the face, and woken up by a dog," Tim mumbles.

She shakes her head and gathers her things. "Bye, Tim."

Tim waves goodbye to Sarah and walks away noticing an optimistic grin on Tim's face as she enters the stairwell.

10

—·—

ECHOES IN THE MAILROOM

<u>Two days later</u>

Jack runs into Sarah again while she gathers her mail. He knows he has to talk to her after the events of the other day. "Hey, it's sketchbook girl!" he says.

"That's right, Sarah is my name. Excellent job for remembering, you must be grim outlook on life guy!" Sarah smiles and turns away.

Jack is acquainted with her games by now.

"That's right, it is Jack. Listen, I want to apologize for how I acted the other day. I understand you have your opinion, which is good enough for you, and it is good that you have one." Satisfied with his apology, he gathers his mail and leaves.

"Wait!" she relays in a huff.

Jack stops and turns around.

"It's not an opinion, it is the truth. Now I don't know who hurt you, but you are wrong!"

Jack crushes the mail in his hand, gritting his teeth. "Oh, and what makes you say that?"

"My parents are deeply religious, though I do not follow. I still believe they are not fools to believe in something. If life is working a job so we can live, then do we truly even live?"

Jack puts his finger on her lips. "I'm going to stop you right there, to say you are a hundred percent correct about your own philosophy is just plain idiotic. I get you need to feel you're right; women are emotional creatures. Therefore, your thoughts are opinions, that's okay; so are mine."

Sarah turns bright red. "Women are emotional creatures? That is your argument. Are you even human?"

"It's just scientific fact."

"Moron, life is not all science and statistics. To say I'm emotional and that's the only thing that drives me is pure ignorance!"

"I can't believe your argument. Seeing how emotional you're getting right now."

"That's because I don't know whether to pity you or slap you!"

They stare at each other, and Jack gives a smug grin. Sarah slaps Jack straight across the face. The sound echoes throughout the room. Jack rubs his face and smiles again.

"Feel better?" Jack responds, unphased.

Sarah gazes at him curiously. Jack knows she's thinking about why he has no reaction. It stung him on his cheek, but he has been slapped before.

"This was fun. I'll see you later, Fight Night," Jack says and turns to walk away.

"Hold on a second." Sarah grabs his shoulder, making him stop. "You can't just leave. I just assaulted you. You should be angrier."

Jack chuckles. "You want me to be angrier?"

"No! But I expected a bit more of a reaction. That slap hurt my hand."

Jack rubs his face mockingly. "It is not the first time I've been slapped by an angry woman. My social skills sometimes are lacking, but if this is the way you greet people the second time, I can't imagine what you will do the third time."

"Next time, don't be such an asshole and maybe the third time will be a charm."

"I doubt that," Jack says. "I should get going. Must put ice on this injury so it won't bruise."

"I'm leaving first!" Sarah says and pushes past him as she heads for the stairs.

Jack shakes his head, chuckling as he heads in the same direction. They walk up several flights together, with Sarah charging ahead and Jack following behind.

Sarah turns around and complains. "Stop following me, stalker."

"I would love to," Jack says, "but this is my floor and you're blocking the doorway."

"No, this is my floor. Get another!"

"I'm not moving. I just got here."

"I was here first, so you followed me here."

"Irrelevant, we just met a few days ago. Can you move so I can try to avoid you in my apartment?"

Sarah huffs as she swings the door open and storms down the hall. Jack does the same and they stand in front of two doors right across from each other.

"Come on! Are you fucking with me?" Sarah says, shaking her head in denial.

"I said nothing."

"You didn't have to. Your stupid face did all the talking. Did you have to move in right next to me?"

"Technically, I didn't have to do anything, but I didn't move in to be close to you. Again, I moved in before we even met."

"Yeah, well, just stop stalking me, okay!"

Jack turns around and faces her. "What was your deal the other day? You were begging me to ask you out, and now what, you're just over it?"

"I was not begging. I thought you were interesting, but now I know you're just an asshole!"

"Why? Because I didn't give in to your little shit test that you give out like candy!"

"Maybe I don't want to be around such a pessimistic shrew!"

"I'm sorry I can't look at the world through rose-colored goggles like you! Not all of us have the luxury of being perfect little princesses who can get men to do whatever they want with the batting of their baby blues!"

"First, don't call me princess. That's demeaning. Second, I'd rather look at the world through rose-colored glasses then live dejected because I got punched in the face at some wedding!"

Jack turns around and faces his door, wishing Tim wouldn't talk so much. He clenches his fist. "You know nothing about me."

Sarah grabs Jack's shoulder; it tenses as she shudders. "Hey, I'm not done with you!"

Jack turns around. "Yeah, well, I'm done with you! I must kill Tim. He talks too much!"

"He only said something about you being punched in the face at a wedding and woken up by a dog the next morning with no context so it's just a riddle."

"Good. Goodnight!"

"Sure, I know nothing about you, but you know nothing about me, either."

Jack walks up to Sarah and grabs her shoulders, looking at his feet, then into her eyes as his somber look turns to a smile. "I know enough."

Sarah shrugs Jack off, still being close enough to keep her sweet scent in his presence. "What does that mean? Don't hold back!"

"It's simple. You're basic."

Sarah's face grows bright red, and she slaps him again. His head jerks quickly to the left and he rubs his face. "Sorry, that might have been a bit of an overreaction." She covers her mouth with her hands, clearly mortified by her own actions.

"Yeah, I'd say so. I'll expound. Would that be satisfying enough for you?" Jack says as Sarah nods. "I know your favorite color is green just by the color of your accessories and the tone of the clothes you wear." Sarah glances at her sweater. "I know you are the youngest sibling in your family, this explains your rash nature and tendency to pout at the slightest inconvenience." Sarah gapes as Jack continues to scope her out, studying the very subtle movement. "You're an artist, but that is more of a hobby than a career. Being there are only two types of artists; those who are famous and those that are not, since I haven't heard of you, you're the latter." Sarah rolls her eyes, but he isn't close to finishing. "You have a decent job seeing as you can afford this place. I've looked at the floor plan of this complex. Your unit is a three bedroom, you don't strike me as a solo type, so you most likely have roommates. Does that define basic for you?"

Sarah huffs, unable to retort for a second. "Good deduction, Sherlock, but I wouldn't call that basic. I'd call that awesome!"

"Sure, think what you want."

"If it's any consolation, I know you, too." Sarah retorts. Jack raises an eyebrow. "You're a stalker. That's the only way you can know so much about me."

"Yeah, that's it." He smiles and turns around to walk away, but Sarah grabs his hand and stops him. "Wait, I have one question, and you don't have to answer, but if you don't, I know where you live."

"Sounds like I don't have a choice. OK, what is it?"

Sarah looks down at her feet and puts her hands behind her back as she glances up into his eyes. "Will you tell me why you got punched in the face at that wedding? Whose was it? Did you lose a bet? And what's up with the dog? Answer this riddle or I won't be able to sleep."

Jack looks at her in bewilderment. She reminds him of a puppy waiting for a treat. "You are incorrigible!" he mutters. "It was my ex's wedding. I had too many drinks, said some things out of place and made a spectacle of myself. I was escorted out by her dad and two other big dudes. He punched me in the stomach, not the face. The mixture of alcohol and sudden loss of breath from a gut punch knocked me out. I woke up the next morning with the help of a friendly golden retriever named Spike. In a nutshell, this is the answer to your riddle. I shouldn't have gone. I could have replied no. But I had to see for myself. I thought it was for closure, but the more I think of it, the more I believe I was there to exact my revenge. I thought that maybe if she saw me, she could share my misery even if just for a moment."

He had never spoken of the reason he went to the wedding out loud. He notices the weight of the memory lift from his shoulders. Sarah stands in shock. Jack had not meant to drive her silent but wonders what is happening in her head.

"Huh, that explains so much," she says, rubbing her chin.

"Okay, whatever you say, I'll see you around!"

"Wait," Sarah exclaims. "Aren't you forgetting to ask me something?"

Jack raises his eyebrow once more.

"Shut up. You're not just going to dump a load on me and walk away. I thought you were going to ask me out," Sarah demands.

Jack walks up to Sarah and takes her hands, placing them on his racing heart. Sarah draws closer as he takes in her scent. She smells sweet, like fresh berries. His heart is racing so fast it is clear she could feel the same thing he's experiencing. Her touch is gentle. Before any more attraction could be felt, he quickly takes her soft hands off his chest. Still with the ghost of her touch haunting him, he cradles her hands, keeping her close. For a moment, he doesn't know what to say. She clearly does not oppose this. She falls into his embrace, closes her eyes, and waits. Jack's lips are just a few inches away from hers, but at the last minute he backs away, his hands still clutching hers.

Sarah opens her eyes as she bites her lips.

"I would love to ask you," Jack responds, "But I made a promise to a friend, and I will not interfere with that until he asks you out first."

"Is it Tim? He wants to ask me out?"

"Yep, and bro code dictates I don't interfere."

"Wow, you really know how to kill a mood, don't you?"

Jack laughs and releases her hands. They walk to their individual apartments, and shut their doors at the same time. As Jack gets inside his apartment, he just hits his head against the door. "Stupid," he mutters to himself in a tizzy, gripping the spot on his chest where Sarah's ghost imprint laid.

11

Portrait of Friendship

On the roof, Sarah is chewing the end of her paintbrush as she looks at a canvas in front of her and stares at Cliff, who is standing in a pose. Julie is sitting in a chair next to her, looking at her painting. Sarah holds out her thumb, closing one eye. There's no wind to impede her. The temperature is perfect, but she needs to work quickly. The paint dries quickly so if she messes up she can't easily blend colors to cover up any mistakes. Cliff's squirming isn't helping. "Don't move, Cliff!" Cliff stumbles a bit as she yells.

"I don't have to be here!" he protests.

"Name one better thing you could do right now!"

"Well, I have a hot date tonight."

Julie and Sarah look at each other with the same thought in their heads.

"Really? What's his name?" Sarah asks.

Cliff stumbles over his words. "It's Be-wil-fra-al, Bewil-fralton the third, we met on a dating app. He's a professional para-sailor. And he asked me to go boating on his yacht tonight."

Sarah laughs as she continues to paint, and Julie continues the interrogation. "Bitch, please! That was the most ridiculous thing I've ever heard. Now sit there and be a good boy for Sarah!"

"Look at the balls on you! And no one asked you, Julie. Sarah, you know I'm telling the truth, right?"

Sarah looks up. "No, I know you're lying. Any parent that names their child Bewilfralton should be shot. Besides, you used to love being my model. What's really bothering you?"

"Why do you need another painting of me? Why can't Julie be the model for once?"

"Please, that little paintbrush of hers that looks like a toddler got a hold of it couldn't capture all of this!" Julie says.

Sarah nods, continuing her painting. "You know why I need you. I told you I need a human portrait for my art portfolio to strengthen my application. And the male form is a lot more complicated to capture than the female form. Be grateful that you are wearing clothes for all of this."

"Your loss," Cliff whispers under his breath.

"I don't think it is. Besides, Cliff, you're just so handsome, and if I'm going to submit the best portfolio, I need the best-looking subjects. It can't be any male to make it to my portfolio."

"Stop it, you flatter me! Okay, I'll do it!" Cliff stands prouder.

Julie laughs to herself as she takes a drink of a beverage. "Wow, Cliff, you're easier to manipulate than most straight men our little Sarah plays games with. It's that ditsy blonde and bright blue eyes combo that makes most straight men melt in her tiny little hands, but all she has to do is give you a compliment and you turn to butter."

"Quiet, snake lady. Maybe if you were kind like Sarah, fewer men would run frightened from you like little rabbits!"

"Everyone knows men are only good for one thing, which is breeding, and if they are scared, they aren't worth my time."

"Girls, you're both pretty," Sarah says, looking at her painting. "Okay, it's finished!"

Cliff and Julie walk over and stare at the painting silently.

"It's not perfect," Sarah confesses, "I couldn't get the nose quite right, but it's good enough." They hate it. She can tell from their vacant expressions it's not her best work, but she didn't think it was that bad. "Crap, should I start all over?"

"No, it's great!" Cliff says, squeezing her shoulder gently. "I would have never noticed the flaw until you pointed it out. Now I can't stop staring at it, but noses are weird anyway. Also, I'm not standing there for another two hours so you can start over. It's perfect. It has character." Julie slaps

Cliff across the head. "Damn, woman! What did my head ever do to you?"

"It was being stupid in front of me. The worst crime for a head to commit."

"That's enough, you two." Sarah stands between them, annoyed by their never-ending bickering. "I'm submitting this piece. That makes ten! So, let's change the subject before I have to find two new roommates."

"New roommates?" Cliff replies sheepishly. "Like whom? Julie told me you were yelling at someone in the hallway yesterday. Was that your potential new roommate?"

"Shut up! You know Julie is right, your brain is stupid."

"Oh, honey, don't change the subject. Who's the man? And when do we get to meet him?"

Sarah grows bright red. "He's no one. I was just disagreeing with our new neighbor, that's all!"

Julie crosses her arms and shakes her head. "We know you, Sarah Reeding; you only get in heated discussions like this with the men you like. You and Jim did nothing but argue for the first week you knew each other. He has to be quite something to get you hot and bothered."

The three argue about Sarah's love life, insulting each other and throwing around their opinions. As the three are having their debate, Jack walks up with a guitar in his hand. As the door shuts behind him, the three stop and look at him as he looks up, noticing the trio.

"Oh, sorry, wrong roof. I knew this wasn't the empire state building."

Jack turns around, but Sarah, for a moment forgetting her roommates, calls out in a childlike giggle, "Jack, come over here. I need your opinion on something. Besides, the empire state building is in New York, you idiot!"

Julie and Cliff smile at each other as Sarah beckons Jack over.

Jack walks up to the trio and responds sarcastically, "Oh, that's right. Man, silly me. I meant to say the Chevrolet building. Yes, Miss Sarah, what is it you need? Hopefully, it's not a lesson on geography."

"Ha, hilarious asshole! No, I just finished a painting and since you know enough about art, I thought I'd get your opinion."

Jack strokes his chin, observes the painting and glances at Cliff. "You're good. It's almost like you just took a picture of this gentleman and captured the backdrop beautifully. Well, I should go."

Cliff clears his throat, catching Jack's attention. "Excuse me, Mr. Musician, aren't you going to introduce yourself or at least play us a song?"

"I'm sorry, my name is Jack. This guitar is not mine, and I am Sarah's neighbor. I found it and was looking for its owner, so sorry, no show today." Jack Shakes Cliff's hand.

Cliff grins at Julie, then at Sarah who is blushing, then he scans Jack. "Hi, Jack, I'm Cliff and that angry woman scowling in the corner is Julie. We are Sarah's roommates."

"Oh, so we are neighbors."

"Does that mean you're that loud boy's roommate?" Cliff says eyeing Jack up and down.

"Yea, Tim works with me; he offered me a spot at his place, so here I am."

"What do you do for work? Are you a boss, Mr. Businessman?"

"I'm head of sales at Pharm-Tech. They had some delusion that I could help turn this branch around. I'm not too sure about that, but I'm trying. It helps to have Tim by my side. But that's enough about me. What do you do?"

"We all own and run the salon Big Mama's downtown. Come see us if you need a cut! And yes, I'm living my dream job," Cliff states with pride.

"Thank you, that's very generous. I never knew Sarah had such thoughtful roommates."

Julie pushes past Cliff and Sarah and comes face to face with Jack. "Okay, that's enough pleasantries. What's the deal with this nice guy charade? I smell bullshit. What are you hiding? And don't pretend we didn't hear you argue in the hall." Julie stares at Jack intensely, but backs away, watching Sarah's horrified expression. "I mean, I'm Julie, and one day I'm going to rule the world."

Jack stumbles back a bit. "I believe you will. I see you are the brains of this operation, and my intentions are pure, I swear. We started out rough. In fact, she slapped me twice, but I think we've come to a certain neutrality. My roommate intends to ask her out, that's all."

"What if she says no to your roommate?"

"That's her decision, I guess. But I hope we could still be friends no matter what the result."

Sarah taps Julie on the shoulder. "That's enough, he's okay." She glances over at the guitar in his hand once more. "We're the only people on this roof right now, Jack."

"Okay, nice to meet you, Cliff, and Julie. I'll see you around, neighbors!" Jack waves goodbye and disappears down the stairwell.

Julie and Cliff look at Sarah in shock as she gazes longingly at the door.

Cliff nods. "I like him!" he says gleefully.

Julie shakes her head. "You'd like him if he were a dictator with blood lust."

"What's the matter, Julie? Sad Sarah met him first?"

"No, he's not my type!"

"Why? Because he's not submissive."

"Cliff, turn off your stupid for two seconds!"

The two argue among each other as Sarah continues to look at the stairwell entrance and smile to herself.

12

FIGHTING CHANCE

In a wide-open arena, two men stand opposite of each other as the rain falls from the dark menacing clouds in the sky. A muscular man in white stands drenched by rain. Opposite him stands a man in all black, his face shrouded by a hood. Both stand staring down at each other until the man in white breaks the silence. "Why me? What did I do to you?"

"Everything!" the man in black shouts.

The man in black lunges at the man in white. The two engage in five minutes of an intense brawl, exchanging various punches, kicks, and acts of physical violence. The fight ends with both men knocking each other off balance but catching their footing as they both struggle for breath. The man in white catches his breath enough to ask the hooded man, "Who are you?"

The man in black pulls back his hood as everything grows black. The word "Fight!" appears in bold red letters on the movie theater screen followed by a scroll of credits.

Jack and Tim exit the theater.

"Man, that was incredible!" Tim exclaims. "Who do you think the man in the hood was, his father, his dead friend, or they'll pull a mask of phantasm? But that was obviously a man, so that theory is irrelevant. Who am I kidding? There are probably a thousand theories on the internet!"

Jack loses focus and looks around. Tim notices he does this when he's not paying complete attention, but he did not care. He's just so excited about the movie. Jack would grace him occasionally, nodding with Tim until he sees Sarah with a drink in her hand. She is as beautiful as the day they met, but it seems like she doesn't notice him. Strange considering only the three of them were left in the theater lobby by this point. When she notices Jack, she waves and he waves back before walking over to her.

"So, what movie did you see?" Tim looks around the room. "Alone?"

With a bit of nervousness, she answers, "Um, Idiots in Love, a heart-warming story that follows four couples, and the challenges that each couple faces in their individual marriages. What did the two of you watch?"

Jack raises an eyebrow in suspicion. "Fight, a mindless beat 'em up movie where the main character fights a hooded figure. The story isn't very good, but it has good action in it. I don't mind turning off my brain for over an hour now and then."

Tim glares at Jack with concern in his eyes. Jack acknowledges him and gives Tim an approving nod, excusing himself and walking away. Tim stands there rocking himself, staring at Sarah for a moment of awkward silence. He then looks down at the ground, then back to Sarah's eyes. Sarah breaks the silence. "So, how did you like the movie?"

"Well, I thought it was just all right. I actually wanted to see the movie you saw, but Jack insisted we see Fight. He loves his beat 'em up movies. His favorite movie is Way of the Dragon, so there's that." He thinks he is in the clear. He doesn't know Jack's favorite movie; Jack just watches whatever Tim wants. It is one reason he was a perfect roommate. Tim doesn't know why he's thinking about Jack when he has to save the dying conversation with this girl in front of him.

Sarah raises an eyebrow in disbelief. "Oh, so what's your favorite movie, Mr. Critic?"

Tim thinks for a bit, then with pride, and an obvious lie, says, "That's easy. Pride and Prejudice; what's yours?" He regrets the fact he did not say 'The Notebook.'

Sarah stares Tim straight in the eye and in a condescending tone.

"500 Days of Summer."

"Oh, I love how those two crazy kids fall in love and end up together in the end!" *Amazing, a movie I haven't seen.* Tim thinks he nailed the synopsis.

"Yes, that is the reason I love that movie," Sarah says with a giggle.

Tim stands there accomplished, lowering his voice.

"Hey, let's skip the small talk, and let me give you the honor of going on a date with me!"

Sarah lifts her head to the sky and mutters to herself while glancing at Tim. "Okay," she relents.

Tim thinks he screwed up. He should have said The Notebook, not realizing what he has just accomplished. "Look, I know I'm not the...what did you just say yes?" Sarah nods. "Awesome. Here's my phone. Put in your number!"

Tim hands Sarah his phone. Sarah thinks, then types away. "So, what are your plans for the date?" Sarah queries

Tim stops as he gets back his phone. "Oh, uh food and uh other things, let's play it by ear." Tim stumbles.

"I'm going to go now. I'll see you?" Sarah says as she walks away.

"Saturday!" Tim blurts out after he confirms she put in ten real numbers.

Sarah smiles forcibly. "Okay, Saturday it is," Sarah says, hesitantly.

Tim shakes his head quickly in excitement. Sarah waves goodbye and then walks away, muttering something to herself.

Tim waits a moment until she is out of sight and then does a happy dance.

—ele—

A few days later, Tim loops his tie, then he quickly unties the tie, turning to Jack, who is sitting on the couch reading a book. "Do you think is this too formal?" Tim inquires.

"Yes, chinos and a button-down are too much, switch it out for a polo and you're golden."

Tim nods in agreement, walks into his room and comes out of his room wearing a polo shirt. Jack gives a thumbs up. Tim then starts pacing back and forth in the kitchen, muttering to himself. *Cyrano De Bergerac real classy Jack, I've seen Roxanne,* Tim thinks, then asks Jack anyway, "What if she doesn't like me? What if she does not show? What if she is late? We are meeting in the lobby in five minutes. Should I head down now, or should I wait and be fashionably late?"

As he continues to pace back and forth, Jack sits up, putting his book down and assures the nervous Tim.

"Dude, relax, it's just a first date, take it one step at a time, and for God's sake, man, pretend like you have been on a date before!"

"You're right, I'm overreacting; I'm just going to go now," Tim says, catching his breath.

Tim leaves as Jack stops him and looks him over. He sprays Tim with some cologne and puts a pack of gum in his front pocket. Tim bows his head in thankfulness and walks out the door. Tim did the pocket dance, checking to see if he's forgotten anything. "Keys!" he blurts out, rushing back into the apartment, noticing Jack pointing to the counter like he knew. Jack could be so smug sometimes, but he knew Jack had liked Sarah from the beginning. But he has to shoot his shot. He could tell from her body language that she's not interested in him, but he called dibs. He grabs his keys, waving goodbye to Jack.

13

FRIENDZONE

Sarah paces around her apartment nervously. *I should have a drink,* she thinks, looking at the bottle of wine on her kitchen counter. *The date would probably be more fun if I was a little buzzed.*

"You know you didn't have to say yes," Julie says in amusement. She is doing her nails on the couch.

"Yes, I did, you know why I had to," Sarah says, walking over to the couch and plopping herself next to Julie.

"Yes, date the weird one, so you can finally date the cocky one." Julie grins. She gets up and puts her file on the coffee table. "It's pretty fucked up what you're doing. I know you love playing mind games with these boys, but this is a little far, don't you think?"

"It's not like that." Julie raises an eyebrow in disbelief. "Shut up!" Sarah wonders how her friend can read her mind so easily.

"I said nothing," Julie says.

"You didn't have to. Your face does all the talking for you."

"And so does yours, my frantic little Sarah. I can tell you're unhappy just thinking about going out with this guy."

Julie gets up to pour herself a glass of wine. "Maybe you need a buzz. If you're expecting a train wreck, you might as well start your engine now." She smiles, pretending like she's blowing a train whistle.

"You're right, I should have an open mind. He loves to talk, so at least I won't be struggling for conversation. He is also very sweet and honest."

"Wow, I said all of that? I'm good," Julie mocks as she lays back down on the couch.

"What are your plans tonight? Cliff and I both have dates. Will you be all right alone?"

Sarah knows if anyone could handle herself, it's Julie, but she still worries about her. Julie put on a tough exterior and often says things bluntly, but Sarah knows in her own way Julie is the most caring and loyal friend she's known. It's one reason they had lived together so long, and even though Cliff would never admit it to Julie's face, he also knows she's the glue that held their little trio together.

"First, I'm going to finish this glass of wine and as soon as you leave, I'll turn on some trash reality show because hot garbage fire is best paired with a lovely red." She raises her glass for emphasis. "You won't be gone too long, judging by how much you are stalling to even leave. And I don't expect Cliff to be home at all. I mean, did you see his date? He looks like an Adonis fucked an angel!"

"I get it. And Cliff's date is not that attractive? Cliff could be home before me," Sarah says, not even believing her own words. It's obvious that Julie didn't buy her argument. "See you later. We will discuss how wrong you were about Tim when I get home." Sarah grabs her keys and heads to the door.

"I doubt it!" she hears Julie shouting as she closes the door.

She finds Tim waiting for her outside the elevator, pacing nervously back and forth. *Oh boy, I hope he hasn't been waiting for a long time. I'm only five minutes late.*

"Tim, hi." She tries her best to sound excited.

"Hi." He smiles sheepishly and holds out his hand. "Shall we go?"

"Yup. I'm ready."

It's cute how nervous he is. *Maybe this won't be so bad,* she thinks.

After an agonizing ride of silence and small talk about music and various artists, they arrive at the restaurant.

Tim nervously pulls out her chair and sits right across from Sarah.

The server walks up to the table. "Hello, welcome to Café Molies, is there anything I could get you started with?"

Tim scours the wine list, lost until he points at one. "We will take a bottle of the Sea Glass. If that's okay with you?" Tim looks at Sarah. She just shakes her head. Any alcohol at this point would be great even if it is a random pinot noir. "Great, and I think we are ready to order. You can start with the lady."

"Very well, sir," the server says, looking at Sarah.

"Uh, I'll take the-uh-ah the chicken and pesto pasta," Sarah says without taking a second look. She didn't care what she got, but she knew in Utah you must have food with your alcohol.

"And for you, sir?"

"I'll have the carbonara," Tim says without even looking at the menu.

"Very well." The server leaves.

"So, what's your favorite color?" Tim asks sheepishly.

Sarah rolls her eyes. "It's green. What's yours?"

Tim took a sip of his drink. "Red. How many siblings in your family?"

"Two, just me and my sister. How about yourself?"

"Um, five, I'm the youngest."

"So, what do you like to do for fun?"

"I like to draw and paint. It's a passion of mine. What do you like to do?"

"Cool, I love movies and talking about movies. When I was younger, I wanted to be a director but I realized that working on movies would take all the magic away," he says with the first bit of emotion he has shown all night.

Sarah realizes she's sparked something. "What do you mean, take away the magic?"

"Movies are individual works of art, which cause excitement and wonder for millions of people. I love that, but if I were to see how it was made, it would take that away. It's like a magician doing a magic show explaining how he did every trick. No one wants to see that."

Sarah never knew Tim had layers or a side of him that wasn't cheesy. "I get that, but what made you go into sales? It seems like two different worlds."

Tim laughs. "That's because you only see sales as numbers and day-to-day monotony. To me, it's a way to connect with people. I get to meet new people every day and hear all kinds of wild stories. Sometimes it feels like I'm living in a movie. Every day has a little bit of magic. How many people can say that about their jobs?"

He is right, of course; she'd never thought of sales that way.

"I think that is a lovely way to think about it. A little bit of magic. That's how I think of art."

"Exactly, so maybe you do get it."

Tim shuffles in his chair, struggling to say something, then he leans in. "Sarah, I have a confession," he whispers.

"What is it?"

"I know you like Jack."

His confession is certainly unexpected, and she takes a moment to answer. When she manages to say something, it all comes out incoherently, "Wha-No-Ja-"

"It's okay. I have known since the day we met. I saw how you looked at him." Tim chuckles, like the situation amuses him. "He likes you too. He said nothing because I called dibs. You are a good person, Sarah, for going on this pity date with me. I'm sorry for being selfish but I had to shoot my shot to see what would happen." Tim shrugs. "Oddly enough, I'm okay with this."

"How did you get this intuitive, and what do you mean by what he sees in me?"

"It's the trait of a salesman. You get good at reading body language. I'm not the best, but you're a little obvious."

Sarah grows bright red. "What is that supposed to mean?"

"Come on, I can't even say the name Jack without your eyes dilating and frown shifting," Tim says with some playfulness.

"Stupid face." Sarah crosses her arms, pouting. "Well, smarty-pants, can you answer my question?"

"Oh, yes, when I first saw you, I only experienced physical attraction because you're like, wow. But it differed from Jack's reaction. It was like he didn't see a person, but something else completely, like an idea."

Their conversation is interrupted by the server bringing their wine, then food. After several pleasantries, they resume where they left off.

"What idea?" Sarah asks.

"I have no idea!" Tim waits for a laugh. "That's all I can observe. Jack is harder to read than you are. If you two were books, he'd be the Count of Monte Cristo and you'd be Where's Waldo, where everyone is Waldo."

Sarah clears her throat. "Um, are you going to apologize for insulting me?" Sarah isn't too upset with the jab at how easily she could be read. If anything, this has been drilled into her head a lot today, but she isn't about to back down.

Tim looks up and with a mouthful, he swallows, "Insulting you how?"

"For insulting this." Sarah points to her face.

"Yes, very pretty," Tim says without a second thought.

"Tim." Sarah stands, tapping her foot, staring daggers.

"All right, sorry! Are you really that superficial?" Tim says with his eyes growing bigger.

Sarah stands still for a moment, stoic, until a mischievous grin lines her face and she laughs sitting back down. "Got you!"

"What? Were you joking?" Tim says, holding his chest.

"Thought I'd have some fun; you really think my skin is that thin?"

"Yes," Tim says, still frightened.

Sarah isn't sure why, but this is fun. She has no reason to, but she has to keep the feeling going. "Don't be such a wimp."

"Learn to tell a joke," Tim says.

Sarah knew this has just begun. "Lilly liver!"

"Wow, 1940 called. They want their joke back."

"The middle school boys called, and they want their joke back."

"Copycat."

"Simpleton."

"Prude!" Tim says, getting a little too into it.

"Woah, too far!" Sarah says, trying to set boundaries.

"You're right, there is a line, and we found it. That's one we won't cross," Tim says, nodding as he whispers, "Fatty."

"Gasp, how dare you!" Sarah says, too dramatically to be taken seriously. "Fat I can lose. You could never lose your ugly." Sarah sits seriously and so does Tim until both burst out laughing.

They finish their dinner as friends.

"So, when can I take you out again?"

Sarah looks at Tim, trying to keep a straight face. "Listen, Tim, I think you're a nice guy and all, but it is just not going to work out. Are you okay with that?"

Tim pouts. Sarah lets out a little giggle as they both press different buttons. "Okay, well, can we still be friends?" Tim laughs.

Sarah nods. "Yes, of course!"

Tim then makes a celebratory gesture as they both laugh until they get to his floor. He then exits and waves good-bye. Sarah still felt nothing romantic for Tim, but she is glad she had this date. She also did not know why she was heading for the roof, but just chalks it up to be women's intuition.

The elevator reaches the top floor and she heads up the stairwell to the roof, where she sees Jack overlooking the city with a black and white acoustic guitar on his left side. She then goes and stands on his right. "Still haven't found the owner?" Sarah asks.

"No, I did, turns out it was me the whole time," Jack casually remarks.

"So you lied to me and my roommates."

"Yes," Jack says without a second thought, "but I finished playing a while ago. Now my fingers hurt."

"I'm sorry I missed the show."

"Yea, great show, lots of people cheering. I take it the date didn't go too well?"

Sarah stares at Jack, who keeps facing forward. "What makes you say it didn't go well?"

Jack looks at Sarah in disbelief.

"First, you two were not even gone for two hours. If the two of you met in a timely manner, it is twenty minutes of commute at the very least, and dinner would take another hour minimum. Since Tim does not know how to shut up, the rest of the time would be filled with his rants. If the date went well, you would have made it past dinner, and if the date went super well in twenty minutes, you would be cuddling with him. So, what was it you didn't like, his looks?"

Sarah looks forward, joining Jack in gazing at the view.

"No, you have Tim all wrong. It has nothing to do with his looks; it was the fact that he wasn't--I mean, we did not vibe at all!"

"Not everyone can vibe like us."

Sarah laughs. Jack picks up his guitar and holds up one finger. Sarah in a flabbergasted tone asks, "What does the finger stand for?"

Jack turns around and smiles as he expounds. "I'm answering your question. In one week, I will ask you out, to respect Tim and give him time to get over you. Judging on how badly you let him down it shouldn't take long, but I also have stuff to do next week, so in one week I will ask you out." Jack turns around and heads to the stairwell.

Not turning back, Sarah stands there in confusion and laughs to herself as she watches Jack disappear down the stairwell.

ell

Sarah, Cliff, and Julie are all doing three different ladies' hair in Big Mama's salon. The salon is small and could hold four clients at a time, plus has four washing, drying, and working stations. Today, they were talking about Sarah's adventure with Tim.

Cliff asks, "So how was your date with the loud boy last night? Julie heard you got in early, so that means he finishes way too soon or you two did not bump uglies."

Cliff and Julie laugh.

"Come on, Cliff, it was the first date. I ne—I don't do that all the time on the first date. And for your information, Tim is a sweet guy, he just..." Sarah snaps.

Cliff snaps his fingers in disbelief. "It's because he's not a tall, dark, and yummy doctor!"

"Hey, it's not all about looks. Jim and I clicked right away. That was not the case with Tim."

Julie chimes in with a tone of authority and sass, "That's because she went out with the wrong room-mate; she wanted to go out with the cocky one!"

Sarah blushes as her two friends and all the ladies look at her as she defends herself. "Who? Jack?"

Cliff, Julie, and all the ladies nod simultaneously.

"Nothing is happening with Jack!" Under her breath she says, "For a week."

Cliff snaps. "Girl, I heard that. What are you doing with that boy in a week?"

Everybody then turns to Sarah, who turns bright red.

"He said that he would ask me out in a week."

Everyone erupts in excitement as the whole room starts with idle chatter and laughter. Suddenly they hear the door open, when all at once everyone turns to see Jim standing in the doorway with a look of determination. He walks up to Sarah, staring her straight in the eye before asking, "Sarah?"

14

OF COURSE!

Jack paces the hall and walks up to Sarah's door, muttering to himself until he gets the courage to knock on the door. The door opens after a moment of silence. Jack looks up to see a tall man with raven hair and bright blue eyes standing in the doorway. *Damn it's like this man was made in a lab*! Jack thinks, gawking at this man who clearly isn't Cliff. His head grows light as he steps back, trying to steady himself. "I'm sorry. I must have the wrong apartment." Jack walks away until Sarah shouts from a d i s - tance.

"Jack, wait!" She runs to the door, giving Jim a look before swapping places with him and closing the door behind her. "Jack, I'm sorry."

"Why are you sorry? You did nothing."

"Listen, I did not intend for this to happen. It's just that last week he came into my salon. We went for a coffee to catch up. One thing led to another, then..."

"Then you ended up with a tall, handsome man. I knew you were picky, but I guess you have a type and it's tall, dark, and handsome, just like any basic white girl." Jack walks away.

Sarah stomps her foot, getting Jack's attention, who turns back around. "It's not like that. He is my ex. We ended on bad terms. It was my fault, so I thought maybe I'd give him a second chance, not because he's handsome, but because we had something. I ended things for stupid reasons, so don't be upset because I can't go out on your terms. He came first. It's not my fault you were too slow on the uptake!"

Jack laughs, moving close to Sarah so he can grab her hands. They were shaking, but he pulls her in close. He gazes into her eyes. "Sarah, I'm not upset. I only asked you out because I'm curious. I'm happy you found someone. Seriously, there is no loss. We don't know each other that well, anyway. No feelings were hurt. It was nice knowing you."

Jack turns away, and Sarah again stops him.

"Wait, that's it? Not even friends? I thought you were better than this!"

Jack turns around, clenching his fist and his jaw. He's trying to be the bigger person because he can't show her his pain. "Better than what?"

"Better than a spoiled child who gives up just because he can't play with a certain toy anymore."

Jack bursts into laughter as Sarah turns red.

"What's so funny?"

"You just objectified yourself."

"That's not what I—Fine, maybe it is better that we don't see each other. You're too much to handle!" Sarah turns around and Jack stops her.

"Okay, I get your point. Friends?"

Jack reaches out his hand. Sarah is hesitant, like she's holding something back. But she shakes his hand and smiles, anyway.

"Friends," Sarah says, as if the word isn't natural. Sarah turns to the door, then turns back to Jack. "Hey, do you want to go on a double date sometime? I know it's weird." Sarah bites her lip, looking down, then back to Jack. "But I'm in a bit of a strange place right now." Sarah hesitates. "If Jim had come to me a month ago, I wouldn't have hesitated, but I met you and..." Sarah stops herself. Jack knew she was holding something back.

Jack smiles and nods. This would not be easy, but if this were a game, he had to play along.

"How's Thursday sound? Martha from accounting has been making googly eyes at me. She's cute enough. I'll ask her out."

Both laugh awkwardly.

"Okay, it's a date!" Sarah says cautiously.

Jack nods and they both wave goodbye. Jack walks back to his apartment, resting his head on the door for the moment. How could she be so casual? He hasn't seen another person in months. Yet here she is, flaunting around some freakishly tall male model. Martha is attractive, but she would not compare. Hating the prospect of playing Sarah's game, Jack begrudgingly makes a phone call to Martha. "Hey Martha, are you free Thursday night?" Jack holds out his phone as excitement is heard at the other end.

At a five-star restaurant Sarah, Jim, Jack, and Martha arrive. Martha is a small redhead with bright green eyes. She's wearing a dress that hugs her figure; the dress leaves little to the imagination, probably on purpose. Both couples sit right across from each other. Jack starts the conversation.

So, how did the two of you meet?"

Jim puts his arm around Sarah. She looks at his hand like it were out of place.

"I saw her reading a sports novel at a coffee shop. She was the only one not buried in an electronic device, so I was intrigued. One thing led to another, and here we are."

"That's not completely true," Sarah chimes in, "First, I was reading Smash Ball, which is a romance novel, not a sports novel." Sarah looks as if she were choosing what she says next. "He handed me a business card and asked me out properly over the phone. He was confident I would like that."

Everyone but Jim chuckles. He remains stone-faced like he isn't in on the joke.

"She's right. Smash Ball is not a sports novel, but it sure as hell is not a romance either. Everyone knows it's a satirical look on the science fiction genre," Jack says. "While also looking at the human races' unquenched thirst for entertainment. The game is just a distraction from reality."

"It's totally a romance. It's a story about how two teammates fall slowly for each other," Sarah chimes in, pretending to push up imaginary glasses, mocking Jack.

"Please do not tell me that your basis for calling Smash Ball a romance is on the B plot between Zack and Julia."

"No, I'm saying the entire story revolves around those two." Sarah points to Jack. "That is one hundred times better than basing your argument off the prologue!"

"You know, the message is scattered across the entire book." Jack slams his fist on the table. "Besides, Zack and Lance have a better chemistry and you know it!"

"That's real rich coming from Mr. Robot Emotions!" Sarah says standing staring down Jack. "The very fact that you are implicating a relationship for anyone means your opinion is moot, and I'm right!"

Jack leans in, about to retort, when Jim clears his throat, stopping Sarah by grasping her shoulder. Both sit down like nothing happened. Jim looks at Martha, who smiles and nods. "Martha, have you read Smash Ball and if you have, what genre do you think it is?"

Martha takes a sip of wine and leans toward Jim. "I did not read it. Nobody reads anymore, but I listened to it. I thought it was sci-fi for jocks. Football on Mars. Besides, I didn't care about the story. I just thought the main character seemed hot."

The four have a heated debate about the book until their food arrives. Sarah stops, exclaiming, "Let's change the subject!"

All nod and settle down as Sarah asks, "Jack, how did you and Martha meet?"

"Work," Jack says, while taking a bite of food.

Jack continues to eat while Martha expounds. "Our story isn't as interesting as meeting at a coffee shop, but it has its moments. Jack moved in a couple of months ago and changed our sales team around in a matter of days. He's so hot when he uses his authority. Anyway, all this to say, I was ecstatic when this guy finally asked me out on a date."

Sarah looks at Jack, who nods as he keeps his mouth full. The couples eat in silence until Jim asks Jack, "So, Jack, sales, huh? Why get into sales? You seem like a smart guy. Why not, well, anything else?"

Jack swallows and wipes his mouth with his napkin, as the two girls look intent. "The short answer is money, but I guess if you want the long and less fun answer, it is the fact that I got my bachelor's in psychology and was accepted into a master's. There was a time I wanted to do something like helping people in rehabilitation, but I would make even less money than I do now. So, I never pursued it."

Jim nods, Sarah sits back, and Martha looks at Jack with more intrigue. Jim then asks the follow-up question.

"OK, what do you sell, and will I know it?"

Jack smiles, looks at Sarah, then back at Jim. "I'm a pharmaceutical sales representative, and you would only know what I sell if you're a doctor or work for the hospitals," Jack says, assuming he has to be anything other than a doctor. Jim looks at Sarah and smiles. Jack notices the exchange between the two and pieces the puzzle together. "Of course, you're a doctor, aren't you?" Jim nods, as Jack repositions himself. "Then you might know my company, Pharm-Tech. We specialize in narcotics and anesthetics. I'm the head of sales, and Martha is one of our accountants."

"We use Pharm-Tech, although we work through another salesman. I think his name is Tim, sweet guy," Jim states proudly. Jack, Martha, and Sarah all laugh. "Why is that funny? Do you all know Tim?" Jim asks, rubbing his chin.

Sarah points around the table. "All of us know Tim, honey. These two work with him, and Jack is his roommate. We are neighbors. It was just a fun coincidence."

Jim laughs, then Martha turns the conversation to Sarah. "So, Sarah, we know what all of us do, what is it you do?"

"I work at a salon where I am a partial owner, but I'm hoping to go to art school soon."

Martha seems perplexed and inquires further. "But as a part owner of a salon, you are making more than you ever will as an artist. Why pursue that?"

"That's simple. It's not about money for me; I don't want to be miserable in a job I hate my whole life. I'd rather follow my dreams, that way I feel accomplished. Sure, it's great working with my friends, but I want to make a difference, you know."

"Oh." Martha nods sympathetically. Sarah's views were foreign to everyone; she was the odd one out at a table of people who were all in careers for the money. Jack observes this exchange smiling to himself.

The rest of the dinner went by great, as the four chatted about their careers and the usual small talk that fills a double date. As the couples walk out to say their goodbyes, Sarah asks Jack, "Are you heading back to the apartment?"

Jack looks at Martha, then back at Sarah. Martha rubs a finger down Jack's arm, looking up at him and biting her bottom lip. Jack pulls on his collar nervously. This woman is interesting. But something inside him did not want Sarah to leave, even if she were with another man. "We are going to her place. Where are you two headed?"

Jim answers for Sarah, "We are going to Sarah's place, so I guess this is where we part ways." Jack isn't surprised but kept his façade going.

Both couples wave goodbye as both set out walking in opposite directions holding hands.

15

IT'S NOT YOU. IT'S ME.

Jim and Sarah are at her apartment sitting on the couch, cuddling. She lays her head on his chest. This double date did not help her conflicting feelings; even lying on Jim's lap feels unnatural.

"Why did you leave?" Jim asks.

"Dinner was over, it seemed like the logical solution."

"Not tonight. I mean originally. Everything seems fine now."

"Yes, everything is fine now, so let's not bring back past trauma."

"But if we were going to go back to where we left off, I think it would be better to remove the stitches of past wounds so they can heal properly."

Sarah sits up and remembers why they could not work out. She had bottled up her doubt, but if Jim were to pry, she knew what she had to do. "You know why I left."

"No! I know a bullshit excuse, where you had a dream, so you felt insignificant. Tell me what the real reason is."

Sarah sits up and takes Jim's hands. "Jim, if I tell you, promise not to hate me."

"What do you mean?"

"Jim, promise me before I tell you!"

"Okay, I promise."

Sarah freezes up for a minute until Jim brushes her cheek. She stands as she swallows the lump forming in her throat. Tears flow from her eyes as she starts to pace.

"I fell out of love with you. I don't know why because on paper you are perfect. I said you intimidate me to mask the illusion that I no longer feel the fire in our relationship. I didn't even know what I felt, but after we were no longer together, I felt, well, I felt good. I was happy. I've never experienced a sense of relief when we were together. Instead, I felt like I needed to be the perfect girlfriend who had the perfect boyfriend. That is the fucking dream, right? It should be, but to me it's not a dream. I don't want to be the perfect wife with children and a little house, who lives a life where she is killing herself on the inside so she could live a perfect life. All because she gave up her life for a man she is now married to." Sarah continues to pace. "I was afraid if we kept going down the same path that was going to be my future. The trophy wife, who never lived her dreams!" Sarah chews on her hair nervously, then refocuses. "First, I want to live my dreams. I do not want to live with regrets. I'm sorry if this is blunt, but it is why I left all those months ago." Sarah continues pacing.

Jim stands up, wipes a tear from her cheek, and embraces her. He kisses her head and laughs as he exclaims, "Is that all? That's nothing we can't handle together."

Sarah can't believe how dense he's being.

"Are you fucking kidding me?" Sarah yells as she pushes Jim away.

"What?" Jim questions, looking lost.

"Dammit, Jim, you just don't understand!"

"Just tell me what's wrong. I'm not a fucking psychic. I can't read your damn mind! No more excuses."

"I don't love you, Jim!"

"I don't understand what you are saying."

"I. Don't. Love. You."

"Yeah, you said that, but why?"

"When we started dating, you were sweet and perfect, but there was no spark. Believe me, I wanted to feel something, but I couldn't. Then you came back. I thought it was the universe bringing us back together, but it wasn't. It was you trying to get closure because I left, but us being back together brought back everything. Nothing changed. I still don't feel that way about you." Sarah tries to still her trembling body. She can't believe she is about to hurt the same man twice. "You deserve better. You deserve someone who will give you the world. Who will give you her world. I just can't do that for you, Jim. You may think I can, but it's not possible."

Jim sits back down. Sarah approaches, but he shakes her away. He pulls a ring from his pocket and holds it up as he stands up. "The night you left me the first time I was going to propose to you because I loved you. I did not know you had lost that spark. Now, I don't think you lost anything. It's the fact you met someone else. I'm sorry I could not interest you!"

Sarah sobs. Jim walks to the door and grabs his coat.

"Jim, I'm sorry. I wish things were different; you really are the perfect guy."

Jim shakes his head. "Don't lie," he says without turning around. "I know you don't think that, but strangely, I'm okay with that. I got the answer I was looking for. Sarah, I truly hope you find what or who you are looking for." Jim puts the ring back in his pocket and walks out.

Sarah throws herself on the couch, sobbing.

A few hours later, Sarah stands on the roof watching the view of the well-lit city at night. Most of her tears have passed, but her eyes are still red. Jack walks up the stairs to the roof with his guitar in his hand, noticing Sarah and moving to her right side, putting the guitar to the side of him. He looks at her realizing she is distraught and then looks forward.

"So, trouble in paradise with Dr. Perfect?"

Sarah tears up as she sheepishly mentions. "Uh, we broke up."

"Oh, sorry." Jack stops smiling and gazes back at her.

Sarah wipes her tears, sniffling as she retorts.

"It's not your fault. I broke up with him. I told him I did not love him."

Jack smiles. "Okay. Fuck him then."

Sarah turns to the pleased Jack, who is smiling at his own joke and defensively states, "No, he's not the problem. I just didn't love him, and I couldn't lead him on."

"How do you know when you love someone?"

"There is a certain fire that is lit in my heart. I don't know. I just feel it."

"There's a fire all right. It's just not in the heart."

Sarah punches Jack's arm. "You would know from experience, jackass. How do I know you can play the guitar until you play? Until I hear you play, I don't know if you're any good, or just a dweeb with two useless pieces of wood. It wasn't until I started dating Jim until I realized he was just a dweeb with just..."

"A useless piece of wood?"

Sarah punches his arm a little harder and quickly changes the subject.

"How about Martha? Why are you not with her tonight?"

"I took her home hours ago; we decided coworkers should not date."Sarah laughs, relieved he isn't with Martha tonight. She changes the subject once again. "So, can you play?"

Jack glances at his guitar, then looks forward again. Laughing, he then finds his composure. "No, I can't play worth shit. My ex left me for a musician and that hurt me. I thought that was why she loved him. He has a hobby that he enjoyed, and it was the only difference. I figured playing a guitar is the most attractive hobby, so I picked it up. I also heard it takes ten thousand hours to become an expert in something. In my time with this guitar, I only logged about a thousand."

Sarah giggles, turning to Jack, who is still staring out at the view. He stands determined and perplexed at the same time. She has spent enough time with Jack to realize that something's weighing on his brain. Having a slight hint at what's bothering him, she uses her next question to get a truthful answer out of him.

"Tim tells me you play rugby. Everyone knows an athletic hobby is far more attractive than an artistic one. Mainly because it shows coordination, teamwork, athleticism. So, stop beating around the bush and tell me why you play the guitar?"

Jack laughs, then he turns to Sarah. "Wow, you sure are nosey, okay then. I guess somewhere deep inside of my mind I thought if I could play guitar, I could win Cindy back. If I could show I have as much talent as that blonde hippie, she would run back to me. It sounds stupid when I say it out loud, but that is what I thought."

Sarah puts her head down, not exactly the answer she had been expecting. They both just stand in silence for an infinitesimal moment, looking into each other's eyes. Sarah's pondering why Jack would not get the hint on why she was on the roof in the first place and is hoping he would make a move. Both stand in silence, neither moving. When she realizes Jack is not getting the hint, she turns away and walks until Jack shouts out in small desperation. "Sarah, wait!"

"Yes!" Sarah says, smiling.

Jack runs up to Sarah, grabbing hold of both sides of her hips and brushes a strand of hair behind her ear, and whispers, "Can I?"

Sarah nods vehemently. Both look into each other's eyes. Jack slides his right hand gently up Sarah's body, brushing her hair behind her ear as he gingerly grasps the nape. The other hand was firmly on her hips, bracing her. Sarah places her left hand on Jack's cheek and neck and has the other on his waist. The two pause, feeling all the tension built up inside of them, only seeing each other at this moment. Jack closes his eyes. Sarah could feel the pause in

Jack's movement as she also closes her eyes, taking in his refreshing musk. Jack's lips inch closer and closer to her lips until her soft lips are against his. She teases with his lips at first, until she moves her lips in a more aggressive manner. He follows as he mirrors her movements in a moment of passion that neither would ever forget.

16

SHELL SHOCK

After the kiss, both stand in silence, ecstatic at the new advancement. Jack stares at Sarah. This has been the moment he has waited for. Jack knew he has to break the silence and says something. "Um, I forgot to tell you, uh, hello."

Sarah laughs playfully, slapping his chest. "Dork."

They both laugh as Jack holds Sarah by the hips and gazes into her eyes. "Hey, do you want to go out sometime?"

Sarah has that look of mischief on her face as she asks in a sarcastic tone. "With whom?"

Jack smiles, knowing exactly what she's doing. "Actually, I thought you could give Tim a second chance, and in return, I could go out with your roommate, Cliff."

"Oh, I think you two would make an adorable couple, so should I call him? Maybe we can double."

"Sounds good, it's a date!" Jack says.

"Come back here, I'm not finished with you!" Sarah Shouts.

Jack turns around and looks at Sarah. "Saturday at five. Do you like sushi?"

Sarah nods as she looks in shock. "Okay, I'll see you then!"

Jack smiles and nods. In his mind, he has two days to prepare everything, but he knows exactly who to call. He grabs his guitar and exits until suddenly he stops and grabs Sarah once again, kissing her. Jack smiles. "Just had to make sure."

Saturday morning is a blur. By four in the afternoon, Jack is on the phone.

"You got it-perfect-how much do I owe you- that's it-No-well great you're the best, Mike- all righty, you have a wonderful evening my friend."

Jack celebrates as Tim sits there watching TV.

"I don't know why you are going all out, man. I went on a date with her and there was no chemistry." Jack scowls at Tim. He still could not believe he would push in front of him to ask Sarah out, then have the gull to rub it in his face. If it were anyone else, he would be more furious, but Tim's friendship is more important to him than any order of happenstance, so he let Tim speak his mind. "But if you say you have something, who am I to judge?"

"You are judging me now, with your judging face and your judging words!"

"And you sound like me."

"Oh God, you're right!"

Jack paces back and forth as he puts both hands on his head. As he grows increasingly nervous, Tim gets up and stops Jack, putting one hand on Jack's shoulders and using the other to lightly slap him on the face.

"Snap out of it, you will do great!"

"Thanks, I needed that."

17

LISTENING TO TRAIN STOP WIZARDS

Across the hall Sarah is in a similar tizzy, pacing back and forth while Julie and Cliff go over the checklist.

"Did you shower?" Julie asks.

Sarah nods.

"Your hair is all done?"

She nods again.

"Did you put on the good perfume?" Cliff chimes in.

"Yup."

"Did you wear your sexy underwear?" Cliff says, striking a suggestive pose.

"Cliff!" The girls look at him, shocked.

"Please, like they will not have sex tonight." He waves away their undignified response. "Lord knows they've been eye fucking each other since they first met."

"True," Julie chimes in, "Do you have condoms in your purse?"

Sarah stands aghast. "We are not having sex tonight!" she snaps.

Cliff and Julie both roll their eyes in disbelief. Cliff retorts, "Is that a statement, or are you just saying that for our sake?"

"It's uh—shut up, Cliff!"

At 4:59, both Jack and Sarah are standing by their doors waiting for the clock to hit five o'clock. As soon as the clock strikes five, they burst out to meet each other in the hallway. Sarah stands in shock to see Jack has cleaned up. He always dresses nicely, but today is the first time she's seen him in a casual outfit. Unsurprisingly, he nailed it with dark washed jeans, a simple black tee shirt and the silver Rolex he always wore. The ensemble was topped off with a brown leather jacket that matched his brown leather boots. Everything was well-fitted and put together with such care, though the most surprising fact was he combed his hair.

Jack grasps Sarah, gently kissing her. "I could get used to this," Jack says, still holding Sarah's hips. "I mean, hello, Sarah. You look..." He licks his lips nervously. She is wearing a light blue dress fitted at the bust but flowing at the bottom with black tights and black chukka boots. A simple outfit to Sarah, but it was enough to cast a spell on him. "Wow, is all I can say," he stammers.

"You don't look half-bad yourself. I see your hair looks like Dr. Jekyll instead of Mr. Hyde tonight." Sarah blushes as she ruffles his hair.

"Normally I go for the effortless look, but I'm glad I put in the work. Because if I didn't, I'd look like a bum next to you."

Sarah blushes as she kisses Jack's cheek and walks away, swaying her hips. She turns her head back. "So, are we going? Or are you just going to stand there gawking at me?"

"Hold up." Jack pretends to take a picture with his hands, looks at his hand, nods and meets with Sarah, grabbing her hand as they walk down the hall.

During the drive, Sarah's curiosity gets the best of her. "So where are you taking me?" she asks, eager to find out what Jack has planned for their first date. "Should I be worried?"

Jack just smiles and keeps driving.

"You know you are a terrible date. The point of going on a date is to communicate with one another, so you can actually get to know each other." She crosses her arms in a sign of protest. "You are definitely not getting a second date!"

Jack laughs as he turns on the radio. "Do you want to have a song? Let's have a song. The very next song that comes up will be ours. OK?" Jack says like he's trying to distract Sarah from her line of questioning.

Sarah gazes at Jack, who is unphased by her words. Not sure why he is being so coy, he has to know he could have taken her to a burned-down circus, and she would have loved just being with him. But a song could be a pleasant start.

"Uh—okay," Sarah agrees.

Jack turns the dial up as the two listen intently waiting for the next song to start. After a moment of radio silence, they hear a song with a strong instrumental introduction. The singer starts with the rock song Streets by Train Stop Wizards. Both listen intently as Jack reaches out the hand that's not on the steering wheel. Sarah grabs it as they listen to their song.

A few moments later, they arrive at an ice-skating rink near the University of Utah. Sarah looks at the building with a bit of disappointment, pondering what Jack has planned.

"Okay, here we are." He smiles at her.

"Really, ice skating?" she asks as they're about to enter the building. "That's your shocking surprise? Dude, I am from Utah. Ice skating is a huge cliché."

Jack hands the girl at the desk a note; the girl then locks the doors behind. "Right this way, Mr. Salinger."

The girl leads the two to the rink, where she replaces their shoes with skates. They enter an empty skating rink that is smooth with a table and two chairs right in the middle. This has been the most extravagant thing that anyone has done for her. With as much as Jack seems to care about money, she never knew he could be so casual about it. Sarah is still impressed. It is sweet and surprising. Sarah does not know he has more surprises, but he does. He smiles at her proudly. Either this man is extremely confident, or he really wanted to give his world. Either way, just being with Jack feels right. The two skate around for a little while, holding hands as they chat. Jack claps his hands, and they put a spotlight on the table waiting for them. After sitting, Jack finally asks, "So do you still think it's cliché?"

"Yes, it is in all romance movies. A man rents out a rink to impress a girl he is courting when the girl would have liked him even if they just got ice cream."

"So, you don't like it?" Jack laughs as he asks her with a calm demeanor.

"Now, I did not say that." Sarah looks down, then back up at Jack and smiles.

Jack smiles as he lifts the silver cover revealing sushi and wine, Sarah's favorite things.

She smiles. "So, do you do this on all your first dates?"

Jack wipes his mouth. "What do you mean?"

"This date must have cost a fortune. I thought you would be more frugal, Mr. I-Work-to-Live."

"Not everything is about money, Sarah."

"Then why me?"

Jack pauses like he's deep in thought. She couldn't imagine what could have been going through his head. "I don't know."

"Wow, I thought you could not say those words," Sarah teases.

"Despite what I said, I don't have all the answers. And with you, I have no answers."

"What do you mean by that?"

"Normally I can get my answer if a girl is going to go somewhere after getting to know her for a while, but we have known each other for over a month now and I have got nothing."

Sarah smirks. *Finally, someone that can't read my face*, she thinks. "What do you mean?"

"It's not that I can't tell what you're thinking. Your face gives away everything." Sarah frowns. *Damn, I knew it was too good to be true.* "It's like this and sorry in advance for bringing up an ex, but I'm trying to set an example." Sarah raises an eyebrow. *Is he going to bring up Cindy?* Jack didn't tense up when bringing this one up, so it couldn't have been her. "A few years ago, I dated this girl, Jessica. She was very excitable; in fact, she'd call herself a dog."

"That's not very nice!" Sarah says, interrupting his thought.

"No, it's not that. It's some theory she has. She compares people to dogs and cats, where dogs are open, excitable people and cats are closed, independent people," Jack says, defending himself.

"She called you a cat, didn't she?"

"Yes, how'd you know?"

"Please, out of those two descriptions, the latter fits you perfectly."

"Are you done, peanut gallery?" Sarah puts up her arms in surrender. Jack brushes his hair back.

"Sorry, didn't want to sound rude, I'm just trying to make a cohesive statement out of my thoughts." Jack takes a breath. "Her theory is not important."

"That's good. I always fancied myself a duck, anyway." Jack stares daggers at her and she just giggles. He gets flustered, but she lets him continue because she wanted to see where he would take this.

"That's what I—anyway, girls like her are all I ever dated. Excitable women who I knew would grow bored with me, so I broke as little hearts as possible. Every girl I've ever been with, I knew from the start that it was going to end. Even with Cindy." This shocked Sarah to hear. "I know it's pretty fucked up, but deep down I didn't want things to last because I knew that if I got in too deep, I'd break. And I let myself with Cindy. I should have ended things, but my mom always told me to open my heart. But what she didn't tell me was that if I did, it would break." Jack trembles. "Sorry if this is too much, but I didn't enjoy breaking up, so I went for girls that I knew would not work out." Sarah grabs Jack's still trembling hands. "That is until I met you, and suddenly I did not know where we would end up. Not knowing gave my mind a calmness I never knew was possible." Jack looks to Sarah. "Does that make me a bad person?"

"No!" Sarah says before telling him her truth, something she never thought she'd share with anyone but he shared so much it was only fair. "Do you know why I play so many games and give my 'shit test' as so lovingly dubbed by the bro community?" Sarah says, mocking the idea, but then gets serious once more. "It's because, like you, I don't want to get hurt. I put up so many walls in my life. Sometimes it feels like I couldn't take them down if I tried." Sarah grasp Jack's hands. He's truly listening. "You know I have never been broken up with. Every time things seem like they are getting too heavy, I back away because I'm afraid, as you say, that I'd break." Sarah takes a deep breath, expecting Jack to back away, but his hands were still. "But I don't want to back away. I want to be all in for once."

Jack leans in and kisses Sarah. "Okay, let's learn to be all in together."

They both enjoy the night so much it seems like time didn't exist.

A few hours later, the two exit holding each other's hands, looking into each other's eyes.

"So, I guess I'll just take you home now?"

Sarah grabs Jack's arm. He looks satisfied with himself, and she says, "We don't have to go back just yet."

Jack drives them to a park with a gate and a road leading to a clubhouse. They get out of the car to walk through the fall-colored trees reflected in the light of the streetlamps.

Sarah asks something she never thought she would ask on a first date. "You know, when we first met, you were a jerk who had this bone to pick with the entire world, but tonight I saw a different side of you. You're calm, and so romantic. What happened?"

"You happened," he says calmly as he scans his surroundings.

Sarah's heart skips a beat at his words. She wants to play it cool, or at least as cool as he seemed to be, but she can't help herself. She wants to know more; no, she needs to know more. Does he feel the same way as her? He must, otherwise he wouldn't say things like that.

"Okay, explain." She nudges him to elaborate. "I know you're usually a lot wordier than this, so this one time I'll let you get into one of your Jack rants!"

Jack looks at her for a moment, searching for the right thing to say. He places his hands behind his head and paces. For a moment, Sarah ponders if she's said the wrong thing and is about to backtrack her comments when Jack finally speaks up.

"First, I'm sorry for the pacing. I do this when my mind gets too full, and I need to utter a cohesive statement. You are nothing like anyone I've ever met, like I was saying at dinner. This piqued my curiosity. I mean- you distract me."

Jack puts up one finger, pacing again, as Sarah looks confused at the now flustered Jack who takes a breath and continues. Sarah feels a shift in perspective. Is he opening his heart to her? Jack has always been a closed book, but something's shifting in him tonight. Sarah's hoping it is the same thing that shifted in her.

He then states calmer, "I guess I should start from the beginning. My dad left my mom when I was four." He tussles his hair. "I was too young to understand. He lost love, but I didn't understand it. I didn't know that was possible." Jack paces more. "Once I was old enough to understand philosophy, I spent a decade—"

Jack looks at Sarah, who saw this was hard for him. "I hit a dead end, all the conclusions seem the same, and I was nowhere close to understanding what anyone was saying." Jack pauses for a moment. "Love dies, and sometimes it's for no reason. This is the conclusion I came to. So, I spent my life just trying to be the best I can, just a drive to do better and self-worth."

Sarah realizes this is not some rehearsed spew he tells everyone, but something from his heart.

He takes a deep breath and continues, "I was doing okay, but then you walked into my life. At first, I thought you were just like any other girl that would fade from existence after a week, but for the first time in my life, I was wrong. You have so many layers and a personality that just gets better with time. I am never wrong. This drove my curiosity and thoughts of you started seeping into my life, but it was not unpleasant. In fact, it was the opposite. It is like you are this positive force that is contagious, making me more of a hopeful person. I know it's a lot, but you let me rant."

Jack paces again. Sarah smiles when she grabs Jack, turns him around, and puts one hand on his face. Jack, who looks away with a nervous smile, grows calm as he put his arms around her, swaying back and forth. As Sarah wraps her arms around Jack's neck, the two dance, looking deep into each other's eyes. Sarah feels like she's floating as she lets the moment sink in, only feeling Jack, her, and something new. The two continue swaying for a bit until Jack stops, leaving one hand on Sarah's hip and moving the other one to brush her hair behind her ear as he kisses her. He notices that she involuntarily raises her leg in reaction to this intense moment. After the kiss, Sarah grimaces, but not at Jack but at herself as she whispers in an angry tone.

"Dammit," Sarah mutters

Jack, turns his head and asks, "What's wrong?"

Sarah gazes at Jack and smiles as she relays, "Nothing, it's just my roommate Cliff was right!"

18

FAMILY FIRST

Jack stands on top of the roof looking at the gray clouds. White particles of ice fall from the sky, adding to the white blanket of snow on the ground. The entire city is covered in a blanket of white powder, making it look like something from a Christmas movie. The mountains turn from a deep brown with hints of green to snow-brushed white. Jack has never seen a real winter before. He stands in awe of the scene.

Sarah sneaks up behind him and wraps her arms around his torso, laying her head on his shoulder. She sways back and forth playfully. "Hey you. What are you doing up here without a coat? It's cold!"

"I've spent my whole life living in Los Angeles. This is my first time seeing snow, and I have to say it's absolutely breathtaking."

Jack grabs hold of Sarah's hands and joins in her swaying for a slight moment until a gentle breeze of frigid air hits him sending a shiver down his body.

"You're right. It's cold, let's head inside."

Jack and Sarah walk into his apartment to see Tim sitting on the couch. He greets them both sarcastically.

"Hey, Jack. What did I tell you about bringing strays home!"

Sarah shakes her head deliberately sending the water from the melted snow his way. "He kept you, didn't he?"

"Considering the fact that I was first to live here means I let him in. Anyway, that jacket makes you look fat."

Sarah laughs as she puts her coat on the rack and walks to Jack, who has made his way to the kitchen. On her way, she passes Tim and slaps him on the back of the head. "Fat I can lose; you can never lose your ugly!"

Jack, who has been rustling around in the kitchen, decides to put an end to their back and forth, because he has learned the hard way that they could literally go back and forth for hours. Jack clears his throat, silencing the two bickering friends. "Okay, that's enough, children! Tim, do you want hot cocoa?"

"What am I? Eight?" Tim responds in an offended tone.

"Yes," Sarah retorts.

Jack gives Sarah a look of disapproval who promptly kisses her before turning to Tim. "Are you sure you don't want any? It's peppermint!"

Tim perks up and jumps up in a moment of pure elation. "Peppermint!" Tim says, perking up. "Maybe."

Jack smiles as he pulls out a bottle of brown liquor. "I was going to add a shot of liquid courage!"

Sarah glares at Jack, who looks at her with confusion, as she takes the bottle out of his hand.

"Babe! There are two problems with your little white trash cocktail idea. The first is that it is ten in the morning, so no; and the second is you are meeting my parents tonight!"

Jack grabs three mugs from the cupboard. "I know this, babe! The reason I'm drinking at ten in the morning is because I'm meeting your parents!"

Sarah glares at Jack. "Jack!"

"Fine, no alcohol this morning!"

Tim walks up to the counter, snatching the bottle of liquor before sitting on the couch again. They both look at him with disdain. "What! I'm not meeting her parents tonight!"

Later that night, Sarah drives Jack through the suburbs of Sandy, Utah, with its plethora of perfect houses decorated with the white cover of snowfall. Sarah stops the car in front of a two-story house with a big front yard and a white picket fence surrounding the yard. The house is framed by two photogenic trees. Sarah gets out of the car and looks at the house with awe and wonder. Jack steps out shivering. He looks at the house curiously. "Are we here already?"

"No," Sarah says.

"Okay—well, whose house is this, then?"

"Mine."

Jack looks at Sarah, running his hand through his hair, but he is also cold so he goes up to Sarah and wraps his arms around her. "If this is your house, then why do you live in an apartment?"

Sarah chuckles as she wraps her arms around Jack. "You know, for someone as smart as you are—you sure can be an idiot," she says sarcastically. "It's not mine in the sense that I own it—but it is something I would like to own in my lifetime. There is something I have never really told anyone before, and it is something that I bet not even you could have perceived. That is the fact I have a simple dream, which goes beyond my art career. I want to live in this house with my husband and two kids. This, of course, will be after I am a successful artist. So, after I am successful, I will buy this house with my future husband, and we will have two kids, no more or no less, one girl and one boy. I will have one naturally and I will adopt the other. Whether they be my kids, biological or not, they will grow up like their parents. The boy will be a proper gentleman who will be something rare in his time, but he will be smart and caring, like any man should be. And I will let my girl dream. She will be smart and wise. She'll know what the world offers and seize it. As parents, we'll let our children explore and create so that they will become strong individuals. When they grow old enough to move out, my husband and I will learn to love each other more deeply in our old age. One day, maybe not our last day, but one day when we are both old and gray, we will lie in our bed on the top floor and he will look at me and whisper, 'that was one hell of a ride!'. We'll look at each other deep in our eyes before we close them to go to sleep. I know it's a bit cliché, but it is something I've wanted for as long as I could remember."

Sarah stares at the house with a look of hope and potential. Jack looks at Sarah smiling and grabs her hand. They continue to look at the house with Jack now knowing the significance of this dream for her.

"Okay, let's go!" Sarah exclaims before they get back in the car to drive up to her parents' house.

Sarah's parents' house looks like it has been plucked straight out of a home and garden magazine. It's a two-story house with walls decorated with pictures of the family. The first floor includes the office, bathroom, a living room with a television, and a kitchen big enough to include a dining area with a table for five people. Sarah's father, mother, and her older sister stand in the kitchen talking. Jack and Sarah walk into the dining room.

Sarah's father is a tall burly man with gray hair who works in finance. He's wearing a brown cardigan over a white dress shirt and khakis. To Jack, the only thing he was missing was a pipe and an ascot, though he said that was more his night reading garb. Sarah's mother is a tiny blonde woman who looks like an older version of Sarah. She seems to be an overbearing home-maker-type with her modest paisley sundress and white frilly apron stained with flour and debris from cooking. And Sarah's sister was also like a clone of Sarah save her slightly taller stature and larger nose, though it was normal sized compared to Sarah's tiny button nose. She wears a periwinkle lacy blouse covered by a cream cropped cardigan that matched her cream fitted slacks. Her style was like Sarah's but slightly elevated. Jack loved Sarah's simple yet stylish outfit with her cable knit cream sweater and her dark navy jeans; it blended well with his light grey Henley and black jeans. There were only a few years difference of age between the sisters, and it was obvious they had learned to speak with one another through certain body language cues. Jack knows it is Sarah's sister he has to make a good impression with. Not only is she related to Sarah, but she is also her best friend and confidant.

The family comes out and Sarah heads straight for her dad, who gives Jack a stern look. Sarah hugs the giant man and kisses him on the cheeks.

"Daddy!" Sarah points to Jack, who looks up at the statue of a man. "This is Jack, my boyfriend." Her dad growls and Jack stands still. "Okay, you boys have fun. I'll go see Mom and Ruthie." Sarah blows a kiss to both men.

She joins her mom and sister in the kitchen as her dad walks up to Jack, shaking his hand firmly. He pulls Jack in, whispering in his ear, "You hurt her, I kill you!"

Jack shakes his head in agreement as Sarah's mom walks up to him and embraces him affectionately. "I thought you'd be taller," she says, looking him up and down. "Sorry about my husband Frank. Having two daughters has made him overly protective. I'm Lisa, and this is my oldest daughter Ruth, patiently waiting her turn breathing down my neck." She looks behind her as Ruth playfully rests her head on Lisa's shoulder.

Lisa heads back to the kitchen and Ruth steps forward. Ruth is maybe an inch taller than Sarah, but has the same blonde hair and blue eyes, though her features are slightly sharper. She walks up to Jack and grabs his hand as she whispers in his ear. "My sister says you're quite the lover. Care to show me in the bedroom upstairs?" Upon hearing this, he realizes where Sarah learned to play games from.

"I'm sorry. But no!" Jack says, backing away.

"That is the right answer!" Ruth says.

Jack stands there for a moment, trying to decipher what just happened, until Sarah grabs his hand as they join the family for dinner.

As the dinner begins, he knows he has to distract them before they inevitably bombard him with questions, so he asks, "Any fun stories about Sarah's past I should know about?"

Frank, who has a mouthful, smiles as he starts the story. "Well, when Sarah was just a little tike, she..."

Ruth waves her hand. "Oh, Daddy, can I tell the story!" Frank nods. "When Sarah was around five, she disappeared for hours, Mom was disturbing the police all day, Daddy was frantic, and I was happy to be an only child." Sarah gives Ruth a look, but Ruth just returns the look. "Anyway, after searching all day, Dad got a call from the neighbors telling him to pick up his daughter. As we all got to the neighbors, sure enough, there she was, just staring at their rose bush. She looked like she was in some sort of trance. And you know what she said?" Ruth looks to Sarah, who just crosses her arms while Ruth laughs. "She said, 'Look, Daddy! Pretty.'" Everyone but Sarah laughs.

"Why would you stay all day?" Jack questions, looking at Sarah.

"I was studying every detail. I lost track of time," Sarah says, sounding like she wants to change the subject.

Jack had only met two other girls' parents besides Sarah's. The first was his high school girlfriend whose parents had caught him in bed with their daughter. The second was Cindy, whom he had dated for six months before meeting her parents. In both cases, he had developed a foolproof plan for meeting the parents. He assumed the dad only cared about his success and what he could provide for his daughter. The mother, he assumed, only wanted to make sure Jack would respect and care for her daughter. Normally none of this would be a problem for Jack, but Sarah's last boyfriend was a handsome doctor. There was no competing with that, so he decided to just try his best. If he could convince her parents, maybe her sister would come around too. Of course, Sarah's extremely blunt mother asked the first question and went straight to the comparison.

"So, Jack, Sarah's last boyfriend was a doctor! What is your profession?"

"Mom!" Sarah whispers defensively.

Sarah's mom shrugs, as Jack smiles unphased by the question, because he's oddly proud of his job and did not mind talking about it.

"I am head of sales at Pharm-Tech industries. You know it's funny because I have a lot in common with doctors. We both sell drugs that won't do any good, and both of us make money from gullible people. Honestly, if I could charge by the question, I'd be on the same level."

Sarah's dad bursts into laughter as he has got the joke that no one else got. Sarah's mom looks at her husband with disdain.

"Frank! It's not funny. Being a doctor is a noble profession!"

Frank catches his composure as he tells his wife, "I'm sorry Lisa, but the boy told a good joke. Doctors are a scam, and you know it."

Lisa turns her head up in disagreement as she asks Jack, "All right, wise guy, what made you want to sell drugs?"

Jack takes a drink and wipes his face with his napkin before responding. "If I'm honest, I would have to say it was simply the money. I graduated from UCLA with a Bachelor's in psychology. I was applying for a job at a rehabilitation center when I ran into a salesman, and once I heard the money-making potential, I chose the better way."

Jack takes another drink as Ruth chimes in to get Jack to expound. "So, let me get this straight. You turned down a chance to help people just so you can make some extra cash?"

Jack smiles, looking Ruth in the eyes. "Okay, Ruth, look at it this way. Let's say I got that job at the clinic. I treat, let's say, a hundred people. A hundred people that are truly and honestly cured. Great, but it's only one hundred people. I figured rich people give more because they have more. If I give to charity annually, I end up helping hundreds in one lifetime. So, I did not choose money to abandon people. Instead I expanded my capability to help. So now I can help hundreds without having to worry about when my next paycheck is coming."

Ruth looks at Jack, who is sure of himself, and she smiles. The rest of the dinner went smoothly and they have an enjoyable time drinking, eating, and enjoying the conversation.

At the end of the night, Jack and Sarah walk out the door hand in hand and as soon as the door closes behind them, Jack looks up, finally breathing.

"Okay, so what do you think? Did I pass?" Jack asks, hands trembling.

Sarah pauses for a beat.

"I don't know yet." As soon as Sarah finishes her statement, Ruth walks out the door and gives Sarah an approving head nod. She closes the door, leaving a smile on Sarah's face, and Jack rubs the back of his neck.

"That means you pass, and I'm going to have a long phone call with Ruth tonight!"

Jack smiles as he kisses Sarah.

19

HEARTS AND MINDS

<u>Four months later</u>

Tim is sitting on the couch watching Fight when Jack and Sarah walk into the apartment. Sarah likes how the room would smell of fresh popcorn every time he watches a movie.

"I guess you finally found the Blu-ray for Fight?" Jack asks.

Tim pauses the movie and turns toward the couple. "Yea, I did. I thought I would preview it to see if it was appropriate."

Jack raises an eyebrow, and Sarah chimes in, "Timothy, you don't have to lie to impress me. You know you will never have a shot in a million years with me. So, it's okay to like your punchy-punchy movie."

Tim stands up and stares at Jack before addressing Sarah in a sarcastic tone, "Excuse me, little girl, the adults are talking. Now, Jack, did you want me to wait for you?"

Sarah lunges toward Tim until Jack puts his hand out, stopping her. "No, you are good. Sarah and I will just watch our movie at her place."

"What movie?" Tim inquires, looking at Jack's satchel.

Jack pulls out a movie that has a picture of four couples. "Idiots in Love. I did not know this, but it is based on a book written by the author of Smash Ball!" Jack says, showing Tim the movie.

"Oh, well, I'm already halfway through the movie anyway. It would be pointless to start over. Good luck with your chick flick," Tim says, with a heavy sigh as he slumps back to the couch.

At Sarah's apartment, Jack and Sarah cuddle up and start watching their movie. Somewhere toward the end of the scene where the therapist talks to two women, the therapist states,

"Love is not a one-person journey; it is a team effort. The purpose of loving someone is to have a built-in support system. It is so you can have one person to pick you up when you fall from the weight of the universe. The universe will throw everything it can at you to tear you down, because love is the only force that is greater than the universe."

Sarah pauses the movie and speaks up, hoping Jack would get a hint. Sarah and Jack have dated for seven months at this point, hitting multiple milestones as a loving couple, yet neither have said the three words that would cement their love for good. Both were in a mental battle with one another afraid to say what they want knowing that it will change the dynamic of their relationship. Neither one wants to ruin a perfectly good situation, so when Sarah asks about the movie, she is really asking about their state as a couple. "You know what I don't get about this movie. No one says I love you, not even the couple that actually loves each other. Maybe if one of the couples actually said those three words, they wouldn't break up."

Jack glares at Sarah, seeing right through her thinly veiled metaphor. It's a good thing because she's not trying to be subtle. "Maybe they know that if they say it, those words will mean nothing. They have a good thing so they don't want to say the one thing that will make their inevitable split even more tragic."

"While this may be true for broken individuals and people that don't mean it, it still means the world to those who have been steady for months!"

Jack says nothing in response. They finish the movie in silence except for the sad part which brings them both to tears. After the movie, Jack asks Sarah if she wants to go to the roof and look at the sky since it's a warm day.

Sarah nods as she walks out ahead of Jack who grabs a blanket and their coats, closing the door behind him.

They lie on the roof watching the clouds drift lazily across the bright blue afternoon sky. Jack's going on with one of his usual rants about nothing. This time being about clouds, and how these fluffy shapeshifting giants fill him with wonder and amazement. In a subtle moment, Sarah leans over and kisses Jack on the cheek. She then goes back to a neutral position listening to Jack and his story about clouds. After a while, she rolls over to her side facing Jack, who is lying on his back continuing his spiel on clouds. Sarah's heart beats faster and faster until she cannot take it anymore, she leaps up and glares at her boyfriend, who literally has his head in the clouds. She finally takes a breath, and in a booming voice with some uncertainty, she yells, "Jack!"

Jack jumps up in a daze, staring into Sarah's eyes.

"What's wrong? Did I forget about something? The dishes? Is your mom coming to town?"

Sarah raises an eyebrow as Jack continues growing more nervous. "Oh, God! Please do not tell me your mother is coming to visit. You know she scares me!" Jack stops himself and quickly changes the subject to an apology. "I'm sorry. Before you tell me what I did wrong, I just want to say I'm sorry for whatever I did. Please don't send your mother!"

"I am sorry," is Jack's go-to whenever he has done or says something he knew he would regret later. Sarah, knowing what those two words meant, quickly retorts as she counsels Jack.

His concern is cute to her. "No, silly, you did nothing wrong; and my mother is definitely not coming over," she says with a childlike giggle.

Jack sighs in relief as he goes back to his jubilant tone. "Oh, okay. What is it then? Did you want to know more about the lazy nature of clouds?"

Sarah kisses him on the lips. She had learned that kissing normally shuts him up, so she adopted the habit of doing this when Jack went on one of his rambles. Sarah then backs away, tensing up. They look in each other's eyes; Sarah, with anticipation boiling up inside of her while Jack is just staring back at her. Sarah finally leans back, shouting, "Dammit, I love you!" She takes a deep breath and then in a calmer tone says, "Jack, I love you."

Jack sits up speechless, as thoughts run rampant in Sarah's head.

Why won't he say these three simple words. Does he not love me? Did I kill him? Oh God, say something, anything.

Sarah glares at Jack with an interrogating gaze as he stands up and starts pacing, placing his hands on his head. Sarah knows when he gets like this his brain goes into overdrive, but she does not care. She wants answers. Grabbing Jack's shoulder, she softly states, "Jack?"

Jack then turns and gazes into her flustered eyes. Sarah looks back into his eyes, hopeful that he has a positive response. Suddenly Jack blurts out the first thing that comes to mind which is a response that's a surprise to them both. "What the fuck do you want me to say!"

"I don't know. What about, I love you too, Sarah! Or thank you! Something, anything, would be nice, asshole!" Sarah bursts in a sudden response.

Sarah turns around and walks away, until Jack grabs her by the shoulder to stop her. He mutters, looking down at the ground, as Sarah glares at him. He reaches to kiss her and then explains, "Sarah, I'm sorry, but I just can't physically say those words to you just yet. I want to express how I feel so desperately!" Jack messes up his hair. "I just can't. Dammit, you drive me so fucking crazy!" Jack takes a breath. "That makes me question if I can handle it but I can't imagine being driven crazy by anyone else!"

Sarah wonders what he can say to repair the situation. She sits and listens to him try but he is struggling. This is not normal for him.

Jack's pacing as he struggles to get the words out. Eventually he finds his footing and continues. "I hate the fact that when you walk into the room, I lose focus and logical capability. When we are together, you are the only one I see. You're the only one that matters to me. It has been this way from the first day we met. You are the only woman that has rendered me completely speechless." Jack rubs his hand down his face. "I couldn't just think of some stupid pickup line because you are different from any other women I've ever been with. It's funny because before I met you, I did not believe in love at first sight. Now, not only do I know it can happen, but I can finally say that it is a completely verifiable fact. Until the day I met you, I thought love was a myth fed to us by movies, designed to take money from our wallets."

Jack calms down and grasps Sarah's shoulder. She notices a spark of something in his eyes. *Maybe he loves me and is literally incapable of saying those words. I mean, this feels like love,* Sarah thinks.

Jack grabs Sarah's chin gently, then backs away. "After we met, not only was I captivated by your beauty, but your mind as well. You only got better the more I got to know you, the true you. And I fell, and I fall for you every single moment of every single day. Each day we spend together my feelings for you expand." Jack rubs his head again, tousling his hair into more of a mess. "Love is difficult for me. I believe it is something that is grown and developed over time, like a grain of sand beaten and tattered inside the mouth of a clam until it becomes a precious pearl. I do not care about the turmoil, because at the end of the day I am with you, and with you I feel invincible. Now, I stand here lost for words because you have made me so damn stupid. You render me speechless with no cohesive thoughts. With you, my mind grows blank, and the emptiness is filled with thoughts of you--your eyes, your hair, your laugh." Jack wipes a tear from Sarah's cheek she did not know had formed as he holds her hips tenderly. "I'm an addict waiting for his next fix. Before I met you, I spent my life walking in this void of misery and darkness, but you brought a beacon of hope and light, because you are so fucking exquisite and perfect. And I feel like a thief of your light, because daily I bask in it and I do not want to give it up. And now I stand here, and I could tell you all this, but it does not matter because I cannot tell you the one thing that matters. I cannot tell you the three little words that you want to hear because those words mean nothing to most but everything to others. I do not think that those three words can begin to explain how I feel about you because I..."

Sarah puts her finger on Jack's mouth then briefly kisses him. They stop and look deeply into each other's eyes in a moment of brief silence as they stand there with thick tension in the air. Jack opens his mouth, but before he could say anything more, Sarah stops him with her hand placing it gently on his chest, feeling the rapid beating of his heart. She embraces him and softly whispers, "It's okay.

You don't have to say it. Just knowing you want to say something is enough."

"No!" Jack backs away. "No, this is not how we are ending this conversation. I'm not leaving until I can tell you what I should tell you. That is the least I can do!"

Sarah puts her forehead on Jack's chest, as she gently whispers with slight amusement, "Jack."

Jack breaks away, putting both hands on her hips, gazing into her eyes, but as he opens his mouth, nothing comes out. Both know that once he says these words, their whole dynamic changes. No longer are they just having fun, but they are a couple with a future. For the first time in his life, these words will mean something. After a few moments of what has to be a mental wrestle, Jack grips Sarah more tightly, then with a sudden burst of energy, he booms, "I love you!"

Jack gazes into Sarah's eyes and in a softer, gentler tone says, "Sarah, I love you."

20

—·—

Back to the Past

Jack finds himself at a bar, disgruntled after another day of work at a lifeless job. He is unkempt and unshaven. His friend told him of this bar with the neon signs with a sparse appearance of people, which is a rarity for LA. He walks up to the bartender who is a burly man with a huge beard as he asks Jack, "What will it be son, something strong? You look like you've had a rough day."

Jack stares at the bartender, looks around, and leans into the bar.

"You do not know the half of it, brother. I like this place so I will open up a tab. My girlfriend left me for a poor musician a few days ago. Turns out they have been fucking pretty regularly. That's cool because I've been faithful, but what does that give me? Nothing. You hear sob stories all the time; you're a bartender in fucking Los Angeles. Anyway, here's what I want, and feel free to write this down, because it will be the only thing I get. I want a shot of your toughest whiskey. I will pound that down quickly, so I want that followed with a second shot, which I will drink slower. After I'm done with those two shots, I will want a light beer to sober up while I think of all the poor life choices I have and ever will make. That will be my usual, okay boss?"

The bartender grabs a glass and pours the first shot of whiskey after checking Jack's ID and credit card. Jack pounds the drink down, then he pours the second as Jack nods in gratitude.

"And sir, one more thing, there's a girl across the bar. What is her story? Did she come in with anyone?" Jack points to a beautiful brunette across the bar and the bartender happily obliges once Jack slides a generous tip in cash.

"As far as I could tell, she came in with a girlfriend who left with some handsome-looking guy. She's been sitting there cursing out her friend ever since. Her drink is a gin martini with one olive. Do you want me to add it to your tab?"

Jack nods as he finishes his drink. The bartender hands him a light beer and a martini. "Thanks, you're the best!" Jack walks up to the girl who is muttering to herself. He smiles and takes the seat next to her. "Should I let you two finish? I can come back. Sounds like you are having a lively debate with some imaginary head people."

"What are you, some kind of hobo therapist?" the girl says, looking at Jack, unimpressed.

Jack laughs as he slides over her drink. "Actually, I am! I found five bucks on the ground, so I bought you your cheap drink. I even had enough money to buy myself a light beer, light because I'm watching my girlish figure, because one of us has to." The girl huffs as her face grows red. Jack looks at his watch. "I've wasted enough time. I'm going to go."

The girl grabs Jack's arms, stopping him. "Wait, do you want to tell me why a hobo has such a nice watch?"

Jack smiles and sits down next to her. "Good job, detective. You found my secret; well actually it's not worth much, the watch battery died five years ago, so I've been wearing it as an expensive bracelet ever since."

"Why would you not change the battery? You can go to a jewelry store and get it fixed in minutes."

"First, it's a Rolex, so I have to go to a specialist. And second, it has sentimental value—it's—I never asked your name. I'm going to need that if this back and forth ever continues."

"It's Jack!" he says, mimicking Sarah's voice.

"Jack, that's funny. That's my—!"

"Jack!" Sarah says as she shakes him awake. Jack's dream fades as he sees Sarah in the small plane seat next to him. Sarah then continues. "Jack, we're here, wake up silly!"

Jack wakes up and stares out the window of the plane coming to a stop. "Ever have a dream that is a memory of your past self?"

"Sure. What does that have to do with anything?"

"I don't know. It's just I have a feeling this place is going to dig up some past ghosts that I am unwilling to face."

Sarah chuckles and kisses Jack, who gazes at her with bewilderment. "You don't have to worry about that, silly."

"Why?"

"Because you got me, and you don't have to face your past alone because I'm right here by your side. That's why I agreed to come with you."

Jack exhales. "You're right, but still prepare for a wild ride."

They both exit the terminal and catch a ride to Jack's mother's house. The house is one-story with a small picket fence shielding the front yard, with a screen door in front of a wooden one. It's a humble home, but Jack, at the moment, is caught up with feelings of nostalgia. Both get out of the car and look at the house. Jack stands there motionless for a moment as he looks at Sarah. "Sarah, I love you."

"I love you too, Jack."

"Okay, let's do this," Jack says, taking a deep breath; the two then walk toward the house. Jack's mom answers the door. She wears her dark black hair in a ponytail making the gray streak in her hair less noticeable. She wore blue jeans and a yellow shirt, still dressing like she was ten years younger. Sarah studies the two of them. Jack's mom approaches the couple, hugging Jack and scoping Sarah up and down. Then she smiles and hugs her. "Jacky, it is so good to see you. You never told me your girlfriend was such a hottie," she says, pinching his cheek, then fixes his hair. Jack just lets her. She then turns to Sarah. "Seriously girl, you are way too hot for my son. What do you see in him?"

"Mom!" Jack whines, looking down.

Sarah chuckles. "Well, ma'am, he's sweet and smart."

Jack's mom stares down at Sarah. "Come on girl, call me Molly. Ma'am makes me feel old!"

Molly wraps her arms around Sarah, leading her inside. Jack follows, rolling his eyes. "Ma, you are old!"

Molly stares Jack down as she threatens, "Watch your mouth boy, I can still whoop ya!"

Jack's face changes as he quickly changes the subject.

"So, Ma, what was it you wanted me to come down so quickly for?"

Molly's tone changes from happy and playful to dark and somber in an instant. Jack knew she sounded serious over the phone. Normally she was better at masking her pain with sarcasm. Jack ponders what got his mom so flustered. "What's the matter, Jacky? Maybe I just want to see you. Does there have to be some alternative reason?"

"Because the last time you called me over so urgently was when Grandma died."

Molly tears up as she hugs Jack, goes to a kitchen drawer, and pulls out a letter. She then walks up to Jack and handing it to him at first, but hesitating as Jack grasps it. Then, she lets her grip loosen.

"I found him!" Molly states hesitantly, "Or rather, he reached out to us finally."

Jack reads the letter, scanning every word like he was encrypting every puzzle before him. "How?" This was the genuine article. He didn't know his father but he read enough of his old letters to his mom to recognize his father's penmanship.

Jack's mom sits at a small dining table in the kitchen and gestures to the couple to sit down. Jack grabs hold of Molly's hand as she reaches out. Molly tears up as Sarah asks, "Molly, who's he?"Looking at Jack, Molly turns to Sarah. "When Jack was a young boy, his father left us. Turns out he met some woman while he traveled abroad for work." Molly laughs to herself. "I always laugh because he went abroad just to bring home his own broad. We fought for days over obvious things, coming up with obvious conclusions." Molly's eyes water as Jack grasps her hands tenderly. "We had Jacky, and we fought for his future. We considered marriage counseling, but there was a glaring issue that had been obvious for weeks." Molly lets go of Jack's hand and brushes his face. "He fell out of love. I knew he did, so we separated." Molly straightens up. "After he signed the divorce papers, I never saw him again. Jack hasn't seen him since he left. He just could not face his son with the way he left, so he never visited, or even graced us with a phone call. When I saw him at the divorce hearing, he told me nothing, and he left forever with nothing close to a hint of where he is going. That is until last week when I got a letter in the mail apologizing for his actions over twenty years ago. I looked up the address he sent it from. It's not too far away. I do not know if I even want to see him. Jack, if you want to, you can see him. That's why I called you. I thought you needed to know."

Jack lets go of his mom's hand and turns himself to Sarah after getting his mom's approval.

"I'm not sure if I want to see him yet. Mom, you have always been the best dad I've ever had." He looks at Molly, smiling, trying to make light of the situation. "The only thing I ever got from him, other than my name, is this ratty old Rolex." He holds up his arm, showing the watch. "And honestly, I only kept it because my mom gave it to me for my eighteenth birthday." He looks at Molly. "Mom, I don't wear it because it reminds me of him. I wear it because it symbolizes your strength of letting go."

Molly smiles. "Oh, that's why you wear that. Son, you know he didn't give you that as a gift. I just stole it from him. It has no sentimental value to me." Jack stares at the watch with concern as Molly laughs and Jack and Sarah can't help but do the same.

Molly grabs Sarah's hands and smiles as she states with some hope in her voice. "No matter what happens today, I'm glad my Jacky has you by his side." She then grabs Jack's hand. "And despite raising you alone, I think you turned out just fine." Jack shrugs as Molly slaps his hand, causing him to flinch.

Jack grasps his mom's hand, then he stands up and his face changes from serious to positive. "I need to think about this over lunch. Mom, do you want to come with us?"

"No, you two should go. Show Sarah your old stomping grounds and the beach. You two have fun. We will catch up later tonight." Molly winks at the couple.

Jack nods as he grabs Sarah's hand and they walk out the door as Molly smiles, admiring the couple.

After lunch, the two walk down to the beach, having escaped the crowd until they were in a more secluded area. Sarah asks, "So, are you going to see your dad?"

"I guess. It's just that I'm scared."

"That is why I'm here. I'll be right by your side for when things get too heavy. I'm your ticket out."

"Thanks, Sarah. I don't know what I'd do without you!"

They both stop for a moment and kiss as a familiar voice is heard from the distance. "Jack!"

Jack and Sarah look up to see where the voice came from. As they look up, they see Cindy and Mark walking hand in hand as they walk toward Jack and Sarah. Jack tenses up seeing the couple and tightens the grip on Sarah's hand. He's crushing her hand so hard she slaps his hand subtly, to which Jack loosens his hand as he stares stone-faced at the approaching couple. Sarah looks at Jack, who seems motionless, and glances at the couple curiously as they approach.

"Hey, Jack, do you remember me? I'm the person whose wedding you ruined!" Cindy says.

Mark snaps, "Oh yeah, I owe you this!"

He lunges forth to attack Jack, to which he promptly reacts, pushing Sarah gently out of the way while he steps out of the way, sending Mark falling forward. As Mark gets up to launch another attack, Cindy yells out, stopping him. "Mark stop! It isn't his fault."

The boys stop, staring each other down and looking at Cindy with curiosity.

"It's my fault. I should have broken up with Jack as soon as I found out I was no longer in love with him. Jack, you coming to my wedding was my punishment for doing something so wrong as lying about love. It probably also wasn't wise of me sending you that invite."

Jack stays silent, moving in front of Sarah in a defensive position, readying himself for another attack. Sarah stays silent, observing Jack. Jack isn't afraid of getting hurt; he just doesn't know what would happen if Mark got too enraged. With his range, he could harm Sarah, even if it were unintentional. This is an outrageous theory but being in front of Cindy brought back some unwanted memories. Oddly enough, protecting Sarah from an imaginary situation comforts him. Not because he wants her in danger, but because he finally has someone he loves enough to want to do this. Jack focuses as he observes the scene like a predator stalking its prey, waiting for the moment to pounce. This will not be a literal pouncing, but a verbal beat down. He is waiting for the right move.

"Jack, I'm sorry to say these things but what you did was really fucked up." Cindy crosses her arms.

Jack nods, still focusing. Sarah, not knowing what Jack is going to do, steps in to break the silence. She plays the innocent bystander and speaks in a Valley Girl accent. Jack knows she is deflecting. *Did Sarah think this situation was too intense? Sarah is a smart girl. She can hold her own.* Jack thinks as he prepares for things to escalate enough to justify Sarah's defensive tactics.

"I'm sorry, we haven't met. I'm Sarah. I'm like Jack's girlfriend, he's so BAE!"

Cindy talks down to her in a tone one would use talking to a child, as she shakes Sarah's hand. "Hi, Sarah, I'm Cindy."

Sarah plays with Cindy, as she continues to speak like a stereotypical Valley Girl from the movies. "Like, how do you know my Jacky? I wasn't paying attention to the conversation because it sounded so boring."

Sarah clings to Jack's arm, feeling how stiff he is as Cindy stares at the couple with curiosity. Jack still focuses on waiting for his moment, as Cindy explains to Sarah like you would a child. "Jack and I are old friends; he came to my wedding. I haven't seen him since."

Sarah, unphased by Cindy's tone, continues her charade. "Like cool, Jacky here is so smart. Did he like use to help you with your homework and stuff? Because he could be such a nerd."

Cindy ignores Sarah and addresses Jack once again, who stands like a statue. "So, Jack, how's it been? How's your 'awesome' job? I see you met another--I mean, how long have you been back?"

Sarah gets upset and readies herself to leap forward, but Jack holds her back before she could launch an attack as he smiles and nods at Sarah before staring Cindy straight in the eye.

"I'm here for personal reasons. Sarah is an amazing girl and my 'awesome' job is still awesome."

Sarah smiles as Jack nods his head.

"Yea, I have been great. How have you been? Still a receptionist? How about you, Mark, famous yet?"

Mark clenches his fist as he stands leaning toward Jack as to look down on him. "We have also been great! Sex has only gotten better with time. Cindy is no longer a receptionist because I make enough to support the both of us. I still do music with my band on the weekends, and I manage The Note, so yeah, you could say I'm a responsible person, because a real man provides for his wife!" Mark replies like he's reciting some creed.

Jack looks at an aggravated Cindy and smiles at the confused couple. "Cool," Jack says, not letting anything get to his head. Jack takes Sarah by the hand and walks past the bewildered couple.

"Jack!" Cindy yells out. Jack and Sarah turn around, acknowledging Cindy. "Jack, I'm glad you're doing well. It really is good to see you!" Cindy pauses. "Also, I'm sorry for everything. I'd say you ruining my wedding makes us even," Cindy says, attempting to say it without being angry. This attempt is halfhearted to Jack, but the attempt is good enough for Jack.

Jack smiles and nods as the two walk out of view. This would be the last time Jack ever sees Cindy. Jack smiles, getting the closure he did not know he needed. After a moment of silence, Sarah says, exasperated, "Thank god that is over. What a bitch!"

Jack smiles and looks forward as he puts one of his arms around Sarah. "Language, Sarah! She's not that vindictive."

"Not that—did you see the way she addressed us in that condescending tone. She's lucky I did not pummel her." Sarah punches the air until Jack pulls her in, kissing her on the head. "She's lucky I defused the tension by going full-on Valley Girl. Although that bitch deserves my foot up her-"

Jack smiles at a flustered Sarah, stopping her and giving her another kiss. She smiles and gazes into Jack's eyes, before getting back to what they were talking about before seeing Cindy. "So, are we going to see him now?"

Jack nods and kisses her once again.

They walk into a locked apartment complex, following a man as he exits. They search the last names on the mailboxes until they see a box with J.A. Salinger. Sarah exclaims, "There he is! Number 302!"

Jack stares at the mailbox with amazement. "Sarah, I don't know what to say. I'm not even sure if I'm ready."

Sarah kisses Jack as she comforts him. "How about you start with, hey, I'm your son?"

"It's just I don't get it. Why would he wait twenty years to reach out to me? What was so important that you couldn't see your wife and fucking son! As a kid, I thought he was some ultra-cool spy. That he was a hero. But now that I'm an adult, the only reason I can see him not facing his family is because he's a coward."

Jack sits down on a bench right in front of the mailboxes and buries his face in his hands. Sarah sits beside him, stroking his back, lifting his head with her hand gingerly. "Hey, no matter what you find out, know that I love you."

Jack smiles, kisses Sarah and stands up. "So, are we doing this?"

Jack smiles, and he shakes his head. "No."

"Why not?"

"I don't need to. For most of my life he has been out of it, and I became successful without him. I graduated college with honors without him. I got an amazing job without him. I learned all the things a son is supposed to learn from a father without him. And most importantly, I met the most perfect woman without him. For over twenty years, I never needed him and I don't need to see him now. I thought I needed answers, but some things we are better off not knowing the answer to. I have everything I need. Why do I need him?" Jack pauses for a bit as he pulls a note from his pocket. "Although there is something I need to deliver to him." Jack kisses Sarah's head. "Please wait here for a moment."

Sarah nods curiously as he runs up the stairs to door 302, he glances at it, takes a breath, and removes the watch from his wrist. Right in front of the door, he leaves the watch and the note. And runs back to Sarah.

"What did the note say?" Sarah inquires.

"It says this is yours," Jack states, holding up his arm, revealing the tan lines that fill the space of his former Rolex.

Sarah smiles and kisses Jack. Jack grabs her by the hand as they walk out the door of the complex not turning back.

21

LETTERS THAT CHANGE US

Sarah walks into her apartment exhausted from the trip as she throws her bags to the ground. She plops on the couch and notices her two roommates standing in front of her with unsettling grins. Sarah looks too tired to care, but she knows if she did not give her roommates the attention they want, they would be even more relentless, so with a sigh of exasperation, Sarah queries, "OK, I give up, what is it?"

Both Julie and Cliff look at one another snickering. Cliff then clears his throat when Julie blurts out in excitement, "You got in!" squealing simultaneously.

Cliff hands Sarah a crudely opened letter as Sarah looks at the two with shock and disbelief. Cliff then explains for the two. "Sorry we could not wait so we opened it. Sorry but also not sorry."

Sarah grabs the letter forcibly from Cliff's hands "I'm going to ignore the federal crime the two of you committed if this is actually what you say this is." She reads it aloud,

"Dear Ms. Sarah Reeding, after further review and careful consideration, we are pleased to inform you that you are hereby accepted into the Academy of Arts University San Francisco, California. Yada, yada official words, starting fall semester of this year." She surveys the letter meticulously, pausing for a moment. "Guys, I got in!"

All three jump up and down excitedly, then Sarah breaks from the crowd and starts pacing as her look of excitement turns to a look of grief. A cloud of realism comes over her and she plops down on the couch in defeat. Cliff and Julie come rushing over to her aid as Cliff inquires. "Oh, honey, what's wrong?"

Sarah tears up as she whispers, "What about Jack?"

Julie jumps up and shakes Sarah. "Fuck Jack. If he is the kind of man you have to worry about stopping you from following your dream, then he is not worth your time!"

Sarah sits up, brushing off Julie. "Julie, I love him. It is not as simple as just writing him off like that. I know it's my dream but what Jack and I have is something I didn't even know I wanted!"

She then sobs as Cliff rubs her back tenderly. "Why can't you have both?"

Julie sits on the other side of Sarah as they look at Cliff with curiosity. Cliff, being a man who loves attention, jumps up and explains, "First, fall is months away, so you have time. Second, Jack is a salesman and a damn good one at that, according to him. Wow, he's so arrogant. How did you two... Anyway, he has a job he can do from anywhere. A few months is nothing. If he wants to transfer, he could do it in a week. So, if Jack is understanding, he could go with you. That way you can have your cake and eat it too."

Cliff then bows as he waves in her face. "Bam, am I good or am I good!"

Sarah sits up, weighing her options out loud. "So, either it's fuck him, or it's get him to move in with me."

Both nod their heads as Sarah jumps up. "Okay, well, the way I look at it, I have one option. I have to talk to Jack. If he says no, then I leave him. If he says yes, then I get everything I want and more."

Her roommates nod as she plops down in between the two and they all embrace.

Later that day, Jack walks into his apartment and sees a distraught Sarah on the couch. He then hides a small box in his jacket and throws it in the corner as he rushes to Sarah as he gently rubs her back. "Sarah, what's wrong?"

Sarah stares at the smiling Jack, then stares down as she replies in a whimper, "Nothing."

Jack stands up. "Okay."

Jack walks away as Sarah jumps up. "Jack, you idiot!"

"What is it, Sarah?"

"You should know when a girl says nothing's wrong, it means that something is wrong, if not everything!"

Jack chuckles to himself as he walks up to Sarah, putting his hand on her shoulders gently. "Yes, I also know you. I know you will tell me in time and I also know when the time comes to just let you vent."

Sarah pushes her head into Jack's chest and sobs. He rocks her back and forth as she chokes up. "Jack, I'm leaving."

Jack releases her and paces back and forth. Sarah knew she said the wrong thing, but she couldn't think of another way to phrase things.

"Why?" Jack questions in a tizzy. "What did I do wrong?"

"Jack, it's not you—"

"Don't you dare finish that sentence!"

"It's not what you think. You did nothing wrong!"

Sarah cries out to a pacing Jack. "Jack!"

Jack stops pacing for a second and peers into Sarah's eyes as tears coat them. This is not how it's supposed to end.

"Sarah, I'm sorry I overreacted. Please explain," Jack says, looking like he's holding back tears.

Sarah paces, fumbling for words. "I got accepted to the school of my dreams, but it is in California so I have to leave. Honestly, I don't know what that means for us."

"When do you leave?"

"Three months."

Jack laughs in a sigh of relief as he embraces Sarah and whispers in her ear, "Don't think I'm giving up on us that easily."

Sarah stops and weeps as she inquires, gripping Jack, "But why-how?"

Jack lets go of the embrace, stares directly into her eyes as he wipes the tears from her cheek and states with assurance, "Sarah, I do not care about the circumstance, because I know we belong together. There is no one I have ever felt this way about before. I sure as hell will not let distance or the minor inconvenience of a job change stop that. And I sure as hell will not be the one who stops you from following your dreams. We will figure it out, but one thing is for sure, you are going to school, and I will support you one hundred percent."

Sarah throws herself into Jack's arms and sobs. "I knew you were perfect for me."

They both embrace, knowing that they would be there for each other. Sarah's happy she didn't have to lose Jack, and she got into the school of her dreams. Everything is going perfectly. Sarah knew that this is the support she wants and she did not ask for as they sit there in their embrace. Jack kisses Sarah's head and whispers, "Sarah, I love you more than anything, and if two people could last the test of time, it is us."

Sarah kisses Jack, smiling through tears. "Jack, I love you, always!"

22

— . —

TWO OUT OF THREE

Jack and Sarah look down at all the passing people from the second story of the mall. Jack then points to an older gentleman with a younger woman as he glances at Sarah. *That settles it. Tomorrow, I see Frank,* he thinks, but the very thought sent shivers down his spine.

"Okay, how about that one?"

Sarah observes the couple stroking her chin.

"Easy, she's the daughter. You can tell by the look of disgust in her eyes."

"Really, I thought she was an escort. What Dad would let his daughter dress in shorts that short?"

Sarah looks again, nodding her head.

"I see your point, but a daughter who does not want to be in a mall with her dad could have worn that outfit just out of spite. Trust me, I'm a girl. I know these things. Face it, you're out of your league when it comes to rebellious daughters."

Jack nods in agreement. Sarah stares at him with curiosity. "Let's do something else. Why are we here? I know you, Jack. There is no way you would bring me to the mall just to play 'daughter or escort,' especially because you hate malls."

Jack smiles, grabbing her hand. "You're right, we are not here to play daughter or escort. We are here to window shop so we can see what artist Sarah will look like. Also, I have some hypotheticals to run by you."

They walk by a window and Sarah points to a mannequin in a strapless mid-length blue dress that looks like a classy cocktail dress.

"I want that one."

"For what?"

"Anything. Maybe that will be my gala dress. Maybe the one I get proposed in. I don't know. I actually don't think my wardrobe will change. I've been to college before. I know what you are doing so let's move on to your hypotheticals."

Jack continues to lead Sarah away as he fiddles with something in his jacket pocket. He tenses up until reaching a spot to sit down. "Hypothetically speaking, if I were to ask you to marry me, what would you say?"

Sarah takes Jack by the hand and gazes into his eyes and smiles smugly as she stands up.

"I don't know. I guess hypothetically I'd say yes, but you better not do it in the mall. This is way too public and not to mention way too cliché."

Jack takes his hand out of his pocket, releasing the box he had been fiddling with. "Okay, what is your perfect proposal then, missy?"

"I don't know. I guess I don't think about that kind of thing as much as other girls do, but I have some ideas of must-haves. First, no standard box. That's way too cliché. Attach the ring to a cat or something original. Second, it must be at a place that has some significance, like where we had our first date or something like that. Last, I must be really in love with the man that proposes, so the man that proposes to me would have three traits; creativeness, sensibility, and lovableness."

"Okay then, do I have all three traits?"

Sarah sits in silence for a while as she smiles, taking Jack's hand and playfully swinging it. "You have two out of three."

Jack nods before he realizes what she just said and releases her hand, standing with a blank look. "Wait, what two?"

Sarah puts a finger on Jack's lips as she smiles and skips away carefree.

"Come on. We both know we were not here to go shopping."

ele

Later that day, Jack is in his apartment talking with Tim and having a drink. Jack is catching Tim upon what happened earlier. "And then she says I have two of the three traits she is looking for and just skips away. What is that supposed to mean and which two do I have?"

Tim strokes his chin as he pretends to care. "After talking with you and listening to your situation, I have produced three conclusions. The first thing is she is ready for you to propose to her. I mean, you will move in together when she gets to San Fran. I think she wants it and so do you, you romantic fool. Second, the one thing you lack out of her three traits is creativity. It is painfully obvious that you are the least creative guy in the world. I mean, even your origin story is cliché, a womanizing jerk turned to bumbling romantic. Oldest story in the book. Third, we are both major alcoholics. We finished two beers and half a bottle of whiskey between the two of us. I mean, the first step to recovery is admitting."

"That settles it."

"Alcoholics Anonymous? What are you saying, Jack? I can stop anytime I want to, you hypocritical Hitler!"

"Not that, you dope. Tomorrow, I will ask her to marry me. I just need to find a kitten."

Tim looks at Jack with curiosity. He then looks at the apartment door hearing their neighbor's door slam. Jack did not notice as he stares down. "It's something you wouldn't get."

"Whatever, man, but if you're thinking about getting a cat, I'd go with a stuffed one. A real one will be hard to hide, especially since she is coming in right now."

Both look at the door as Sarah walks in, greeting the two boys. She then walks up to Jack and kisses his cheek. "Hey, honey!" She then looks at Tim, pretending to tip an imaginary hat. "Doofus."

Tim leans over, pretending to whisper, "Please, Jack is sitting right there, save the name calling for when he is gone."

"Why, don't you want your muse to see you cry, princess?"

"Ha, jokes on you. He already has you, Wicked Witch of the East."

"That's of the west to you, Dorothy."

"I'm sorry. Did I call you a witch? I meant a flying monkey."

"Well, at least I have a brain scarecrow."

"That shirt makes you look fat!"

"Fat I can lose. You can't lose your ugly."

The two stare each other down for a second until Jack kisses Sarah and interrupts. "Tim, we are going to bed now. It's late, do you want another shot?"

"No, I'm good. Goodnight, Jack!" He then sticks out his tongue at Sarah. "Elphaba."

Sarah glares back and lunges toward Tim, as Jack grabs her hand, leading her to his bedroom, whispering, "Let it go, you have all morning to riff back and forth."

Sarah smiles and looks back at Tim, sticking her tongue out.

The next evening, Jack and Sarah are skating at the rink they had their first date in. Jack has a stuffed cat in his pocket. The two enjoy each other's company as Jack starts a conversation.

"Sarah, you know I love you, right?"

"Of course, I do, and I love you."

"Well, Sarah, I don't want to love anyone else. I want to be with you for the rest of my life."

Jack gets down on one knee until Sarah stops him.

"Hold that thought."

"What's wrong?" Jack asks.

"Jack, I love you with all my heart and I would love to marry you! But-"

"But what?" Jack stands holding her hips.

"I want to wait till after I finish school." Jack drops his head, closing his eyes. Sarah smiles, kissing him. "Besides,

I know you haven't talked to my father yet. The last time a man talked to him, he called me that day crying so uncontrollably I couldn't understand a word he said." Sarah chuckles, kissing Jack's cheek and playfully skates away.

23

I'm the Baby?

Jack sits in front of Frank in his office, nervous as he studies the giant man's face. He can't tell what he's thinking as he just sits there. This makes Jack feel like he is in the middle of an interrogation.

Although torture to him would be sweet relief in comparison to the agonizing silence.

"Let me get this straight. You want my blessing to marry my daughter?" Frank says, finally breaking the silence but not the tension, as Jack nods nervously. Frank smiles. "And you want to keep my blessing for as long as Sarah is in college? That could take two years or six until you can finally ask her when she gets that degree."

"Yes, sir."

Frank bursts out laughing. "You sure are an odd boy!" Frank leans into Jack. "Of course, you have my blessing, especially knowing I won't have to give up my daughter for many years," Frank says. "Besides, I can't think of a better bloke to take my daughter's hand. I admire your patience, boy. If it were me, I'd go crazy!"

"Thank you, sir!" Jack says, jumping up and shaking Frank's hand.

"While we're on the topic of marrying my daughters, you have anyone in mind for my daughter Ruth? She's wild, but she needs to settle down with a nice boy."

Jack smiles. "My roommate Tim is single."

"No!" Ruth screams from behind the door. She runs off looking guilty.

Jack realizes Ruth could leak this conversation to Sarah. Not wanting to expose his intentions yet, he chases Ruth up the stairs, waving goodbye to Frank.

As he goes upstairs, he sees Ruth on the phone.

"Sarah, you will never guess what Jack just asked Dad!"

Sarah's voice could be heard at the other end as Jack quickly jumps on top of Ruth, covering her mouth with his one hand, getting hold of her phone. "Nothing. I just needed to know what motor oil he uses! Love you, bye!" He hangs up the phone, still holding Ruth's mouth, until Ruth bites hard on his hand. "Ow, dammit! You bit me!" Jack screams, backing off Ruth.

"That's what you get for jumping a lady!"

"I didn't jump a lady. I jumped on you." Ruth crawls over to Jack and bites his hand again. "What's wrong with you woman! Are you rabid?"

"And that's what you get for insulting a lady!"

"Okay, fine. Sorry!" Jack sits against one wall and Ruth sits against the other, breathing heavy from their wrestle. "Listen, I don't know what you heard, but I'm going to need you to not tell Sarah."

"Are you asking me to lie to my sister!"

"No, I'm asking you to keep a secret for your future brother."

"Who's that?" Ruth says sarcastically.

"Hilarious!" Jack sits up, holding his hand. "I'm serious, Sarah is leaving for college soon. And I can't have a future blessing distract her from going." Jack knew this would be hard for Ruth, but he couldn't have this little meeting stop her from living her dream.

"Okay, I won't tell her."

"Thank you, Ruth, this—"

"Let me finish, Casanova!" Ruth says, interrupting. "I won't tell on two conditions. The first is you never suggest that I date your roommate ever again! And second, you ask for my blessing."

"I don't know. Tim's a nice guy." Ruth grabs her phone, threatening to dial. Jack franticly responds. "Sorry, it was a joke!" Jack then thinks for a beat. "The Tim thing I get, but why do you want me to ask for your blessing?"

"Because a father's blessing is tradition, yes, but a sister's blessing is the most powerful." Ruth pauses for a beat. "It is like if the pope were to baptize a baby."

"So, in this scenario, you're the pope and I'm—"

"The baby!" Ruth interrupts. "Wow, Sarah was right, you really are smart."

"Ruth, may I have your blessing to marry your sister?"

Ruth gets up, stroking her chin. "I don't know. I could do better in terms of brothers-in-law, although I could also do worse."

"Ruth, look at me," Jack says, jumping up and grasping her shoulders. "I love your sister more than anything in this world." He stares deep into Ruth's eyes. "The very thought of being without her kills me!" Jack lets go of Ruth's shoulders. "If I don't get your blessing, then I will beg you every day if I have to. Don't forget, I have years to spare."

"Okay, you have my blessing, young baby!" Ruth pretends to cry. "They just grow up so fast."

Jack embraces Ruth. "Thank you so much!"

"You're welcome. I just have one more request." Jack lets go of Ruth, looking at her curiously, but Ruth just grins like she has just finished her plans for world domination. "I want to spend the day with you. I want to see if you really have what it takes to be my brother-in-law."

"That's it! I can't wait. Besides, Sarah said I need to make more of an effort to spend time with you, anyway." Jack observes Ruth, who is grinning. "I guess it's a date, then."

Ruth just grins. Jack ponders what is going on inside her brain, but he knows that this can only strengthen their relationship. After all, he hadn't met a closer pair of sisters than the Reeding girls.

24

***

TO PAINT A TREE

Sarah is sitting on the roof chewing on her paintbrush as she stares at her tree painting. She tries to focus on the clear blue sky but all she can focus on is the fact that the painting causes her so much pain. This painting that she originally submitted as part of her portfolio to the school. Despite all the turmoil she's attached to this piece, she knows there is something there, but the frustrating part is she doesn't know what it is. *What's your story?* she thinks, biting on her paintbrush.

Jack sneaks behind her, putting his hands over her eyes. "Guess who?"

"Jack, I don't have time for games. I'm struggling to finish this piece."

"Sorry." Jack studies the painting. "What were you thinking of doing with it? Looks good to me."

"You dunce, this is the most incomplete painting I've ever done!" Jack puts his hands up in surrender. Sarah did not mean to yell, so she backtracks. "I'm sorry. I'm just stressed." Sarah stands and kisses Jack properly, greeting him.

"I'm no artist, but is there anything I can help you with?"

"If you insist, what story does this painting tell you?"

"It's not telling me anything; it's a painting."

Sarah slaps Jack's arm. "This is no time to be funny, be honest with me!"

"Sorry. I see a tree, it's big, so that means it's hundreds of years old. So, it's probably seen some shit."

"What kind of shit? Be more specific, Jack."

Jack tussles his hair. "Shit like its friends have been chopped down by guys in flannels, lightning striking down others. It has probably seen life end and begin. It's seen thousands of sunrises and starry nights. I don't know—tree stuff."

"Thanks for trying." Sarah chuckles as she kisses his cheek. "What did you need to see me for?"

"Oh, yeah, your sister wants to spend the day with me. I just wanted to make sure you were okay with that?"

Sarah grins. She loves that Jack is putting in the time to get to know her sister. "I am more than okay with that. In fact, I demand you do!" Sarah says. "Besides, I need to focus on this painting, so I have no time for you, sorry." Sarah loves spending time with Jack, but he is a major distraction. When she is with him all she wants to do is just

be with him. His spending the day with Ruth may give her
the time to discover her painting's story.

"Okay, love you," Jack says as he kisses her.

"Love you too." She waves to Jack as he exits and she
focuses on the painting, muttering to herself, "Tree, tree,
leaves, wood, huh wood, wood, acoustic guitar, music,
music notes. Music!" Sarah excitingly paints one music
note on the canvas. "That's it! It's not just some tree!"
Sarah jumps up, celebrating. "Take that, Mrs. Harding!"

Later that day, Sarah is in her parents' house in her old
room. Ruth sneaks up behind her.

"Hey, little sister!" Ruth exclaims, causing Sarah to paint
a streak on her painting.

"Dammit Ruthie! Look what you made me do!"

"Sorry!" Ruth examines the painting. "I'm sure you can
paint over that."

"That's not the point, Ruthie." Sarah blends in the
smudge in the painting. "What are you doing here, anyway?"

"I live here, saving up to travel the world, remember?"
Ruth sits on the bed. "The real question is what are you
doing here? Don't you have your own apartment to angst
in?"

"My apartment is distracting. I need silence to finish."

"Is it the apartment or is it Jack taking up all that free space in your brain?"

Sarah scowls at Ruth.

"Don't frown at me, young lady!" Ruth says. "You and I both know since you started dating that boy, you've been distracted."

Sarah turns away from Ruth. She knows Ruth is right but she did not want to give her an inch. "So!" she says, not wanting to hear what Ruth will probably tell her.

"Sarah, I love you, and I think Jack is the best man you ever dated. I will always root for Sack." Ruth makes a face of disgust at the couple's name. "Let's just go with Jarah. That's better."

"Ruthie, get to the but already."

"Okay, you asked for it." Ruth stands on the bed and shakes her butt in front of Sarah.

Sarah laughs. "Ruthie, you tease!"

Ruth sits back down, a bit more somber. "All right, that's enough dicking around. You can't move in with Jack."

"Why?"

"I know it's not what you want to hear, and like I said, I'm not saying to break up with him." Ruth walks up to Sarah, hugging her from behind. "But you and I both know if you truly want to succeed as an artist, you can't be distracted." Ruth walks around, standing in front of Sarah.

"But Ruthie—"

"But nothing! You know I'm right."

"I know you are," Sarah says as she weeps in Ruth's arms.

"There, there." Ruth grasps Sarah's shoulders, looking her in the eyes, glistening with tears. "Besides, I don't think distance is going to get between the both of you." Ruth hugs Sarah, getting her shirt wet from her tears.

25

ROOFTOP

A few days later, Jack and Sarah are back to normal, cuddling in Sarah's apartment until Julie and Cliff barge in as Julie announces, "All right, we are home, so that's enough of your happy couple act."

"If it's an act, why are we doing it when we're alone?" Jack says smugly.

Julie forces herself between the couple and scowls at Jack. "Don't sass me boy!"

Jack just looks away as the three sit there awkwardly. Cliff, who has been rummaging through the cupboard searching for a snack, breaks the silence. "Okay. What Julie is trying to say is that we want to throw you a going away party, or at least congratulations for getting into your dream school party!"

Sarah jumps up in a grimace. "Cliff, Julie, I told you two no parties! You know I hate them, and people always make a mess, and besides that I told you all I don't want you to make a big deal, I just want a quiet send-off."

Julie jumps up, dragging the dejected Sarah to the kitchen to join Cliff, leaving Jack sitting on the couch alone as Julie explains, "I know you said something small, but we are going to do this, and we are still going to say a small, more personalized goodbye when you actually leave."

The three start a back-and-forth conversation about the party that went by too fast for any human to understand, with all of them talking over each other in different fluctuations. Jack glances back from the couch and questions. "Hey, guys, don't I get a say in this matter?"

All three stop and simultaneously say, "No!"

On the day of the party, Jack and Sarah look at Sarah's door and Jack grabs her hand. "Don't worry, Tim is in there and he's enjoying himself. He texted me saying it's 'lit.' I don't know what that means, but I'm sure he's not using that phrase right."

"Yea, but Tim could enjoy himself watching a professional golf game."

"I heard those can get pretty lit."

Both look at each other and laugh as Sarah stops and tells Jack.

"Okay, I will try to enjoy myself, but as soon as I've had enough, our safe word will be 'Rooftop.' As soon as I say that, you and I will go to the roof."

"Sounds good, shall we go in, my lady?" Jack holds out his arm. Sarah smiles and wraps her arm into his as they walk into the party. The party's lively; there's music playing in the background, and it smells of alcohol and incense. Sarah's apartment appears more open, as people were dancing in some open corners. It's filled with people. Tim's walking around, getting rejected left and right; Sarah and Jack enjoy watching the man try so hard. As people ask Sarah about her college, her face lights up with excitement. Eventually Jack leaves Sarah talking with Ruth, who got there before them. He talks with Cliff against the counter. With a beer in his hand, he leans against the counter, observing Sarah.

Cliff just laughs as he jests at Jack. "Wow, honey, you are so straight!"

"What makes you say that?"

"First off, you grab a beer from the bottle. Second, you lean and slouch like a man who sleeps with women and thinks he owns the place, and third, you are so obviously enamored with my roommate who is so cookie cutter white girl, it's not even funny."

"Okay, touché, my friend, but I can't help but be enamored. I love her."

"Aww, you two are so cute together it makes me want to hurl."

"Come on, you've never had some guy you were in love with?"

"I have, but it's been so long I can't remember. Unlike you horny straight men, I can keep it in my pants until I find the one!"

"That's funny. I always thought it was the opposite with gay men. Unlike women, you guys have fewer criteria. I thought for you, it was does he have a dick? Yes? Okay, it's on."

"Don't be sexist," Cliff says exaggeratedly.

They both laugh at the concept.

"You really love her. You're not lying. Even I can see she is the only one you paid any attention to since you walked in."

"Yea, I do, but enough about me. What about you? Any cute guys catching your attention here?"

"Not at all, the guys here are either straight or ones I've already slept with."

"Cliff, you slut."

"Hey, you have no room to talk. Sarah told me your number. Even if I were straight, I'd get myself tested after that many partners."

Jack takes a sip of his beer as he mumbles, "I did, and I'm safe."

Both laugh, until Cliff notices Tim as he makes his way to Julie. Cliff taps Jack on the shoulder.

"Speaking of straight, let's watch your little friend strike out trying to ask Julie out."

Tim approaches Julie with confidence. "Hey, girl, come here often?"

"Tim, I live here, you goob!"

"Oh, I hadn't noticed. So how about you give me a tour of your bedroom?" Tim says, leaning in closer.

"Oh, sweetie, how do I put this gently? First off, you're not my type. Second, I wouldn't fuck you if you were the last man on the planet, and lastly, even if I were drunk and desperate enough, you could not handle me," she says, backing away.

"I did not hear a no."

"Wow, you are special. Okay then, no! Never! Nein! Nilch! Not a chance in your pathetic life!" She puts her hand in his face, walking away.

"I get it, still friends."

"Sure."

Tim reaches out and gives her hand a shake. Julie then walks up to Jack and Cliff as they all watch Tim skip joyfully away.

"How does a man like that keep going after being rejected by every girl at this party?"

Jack points to Tim who is dancing like no one is watching, flailing back and forth like a fish gasping for air, without a care in the world.

"You see, Julie, Tim is what some will call an optimist. He sees the good and the possibilities in people and situations no matter what. Honestly, it is his inability to look at negatives that makes him a great salesman. As for dating, he views it as a numbers game; for every thousand no's he gets, he is bound to get one yes. He doesn't see it as failing, he sees it as one step closer to that yes. And you just got him five steps closer."

Julie smiles and then stands on Jack's other side. "Wow, Sarah's right. You are observant, and it looks like a little of Tim has rubbed off on you."

"I live with the boy. He's part of the reason I'm the man I've become today, but Sarah is the main reason for that. Tim may have opened my mind to optimism, but Sarah is the one that opened my heart to it."

He smiles as he notices Sarah laughing and enjoying herself. Julie and Cliff smile. Cliff studies Jack's face. "Okay, I'm going to say I like you better than any other boyfriend that she has ever had!"

"I second that motion!" Julie chimes in an unusual cheery tone.

Cliff and Julie both hug Jack on their respective sides. Sarah walks up to the three and grabs Jack by the arm and as Jack waves goodbye, she states, "Rooftop!"

The two make their way to the roof and sit on the bench where Jack first kissed Sarah.

"Listen, Jack, I don't want you to come with me to San Francisco. I can't ask you to give up your job and start over; it is not fair to you."

Jack jumps up and grabs Sarah's hand.

"Sarah, I'm not giving up anything. I will lose a couple thousand a year, but it is nothing. We can't survive."

"Jack, you know I love you."

"I love you too, that is why I'm making this sacrifice."

"It's not that, Jack. I think you're a distraction."

"What do you mean?"

"When I'm with you, I feel great and I love it, but I also don't focus on my art. The day you spent with my sister, I got more art done than in the months we have been dating. I don't want to break up, but I do not want you to come with me. Does that make sense?"

"Sarah, remember when I said distance will not separate us, I meant we would figure this out. I understand you need to do this for yourself. I won't get in your way."

Sarah kisses Jack. "Okay, let's come up with a game plan. How will we do this long-distance thing?"

"OK, here's the plan. I will write you a letter twice every month. Just to give you a recap, we FaceTime on the weekends. I will visit on some holidays, and you can visit on others. And if you ever miss me, you can text or call. I will not make any first contact, so I do not distract you. I love you. Distance will not stop us."

"I like that plan. And I love you too."

Both kiss and embrace one another.

The next two weeks go by in a flash with packing, goodbyes and getting stuff together for Sarah's school. Sarah, Jack, Cliff, Ruth, and Julie all have mimosas and brunch before Sarah needs to leave to catch her flight. At the airport, there's a lot of crying and good lucks as she embraces her roommates, sister, and then Jack. As she holds on to Jack, she whispers, "I love you."

"And I love you, always," Jack states, kissing her forehead.

Both hold on for a while longer. Jack kisses her like it is the last kiss he will ever give her. It will not be, but he needs this one to last. Everyone waves goodbye as Sarah disappears into the airport.

26

— · —

LETTERS

September 4

Dear Jack,

I am absolutely enjoying this whole letter writing thing. It is so old school, but that is to be suspected of a man as old-fashioned as you. I swear you were born fifty years too late, but that is one thing I love about you. I have been adjusting to California life just fine, and I do not understand why you hate it so much. The bay is beautiful. I love it when the fog rolls over the city. I know it's kind of touristy, but I've sketched like a hundred pictures of the Golden Gate Bridge. School has been amazing. My professors and classmates are all so supportive. I am on the older side of the students.

At first I thought that being slightly older was going to be a bit of a disadvantage, but we are all artists and have a remarkably similar mindset. It is so beautiful to have a whole school of people who see the world the same way I do. On my first day, I met a guy named Jeremy. He was so helpful and showed me around. The campus is bigger than I expected, but I love it.

Anyway, that's enough about me, what about you? How's work? Are you still in touch with Julie and Cliff? Most important, how are you doing emotionally? I will not lie, I've been missing you like crazy and am counting down the days until I can see you again.

Love you always,

Sarah.

PS. Do not worry about Jeremy. He is nothing but a friend and our relationship could not be any more platonic. He reminds me of a tall version of Tim.

September 12

Dear Sarah,

I am so glad to hear that you are doing great. Things here have been great, but they would be better if you were here with me. I have been focusing on work and training Tim so he can eventually take my place so I can confidently leave my job with no regrets. I have been using the spare time to complete my master's degree. It turns out that I only need a year's worth of credits to get my master's in psychology.

So next year I can start looking for a job doing something that will make a difference.

Julie and Cliff are doing great. They moved to a smaller apartment to save some money. I see them when I get my hair cut, but they are doing great. We only talk about you when I see them.

As for my emotional state, I am doing good. I have learned to open up more and to dream big, and that is because of you. I learned that from you. I also miss you a ton, and I cannot wait to visit you after this semester is over. Every second that goes by is one second closer to you, and that's what keeps me going.

Love you always,

Jack.

PS: I am not worried about Jeremy. I trust you and know you are not the cheating type. I love you too much to worry.

February 6

Dear Jack,

I am going to keep this brief, because you are coming over in less than a week, but I can't wait to see you. There are so many things I want to tell you, but most importantly, there are things I need to tell you. I am not expecting a return letter because I will see you before that. I miss you, but not for too much longer.

    Love always,
    Sarah

27

My Heart in San Francico

Jack sits in a chair in a salon getting his haircut from Cliff as they engage in casual conversation with Julie standing next to him, cutting another woman's hair.

"So, I'm flying out to see Sarah tomorrow. Is there anything you guys want to give her or for me to pick up while I'm there?"

Cliff studies Jack's hair and starts to cut it methodically as he answers Jack.

"Jack, honey we've already mailed Sarah everything we needed to, so don't worry about us. But if you can get some Ghirardelli chocolate that would be great!"

"Okay, I can make that happen."

He and Cliff laugh as Julie gives Cliff an intimidating look. He clears his throat and finishes Jack's haircut. Jack pays and says his goodbyes. Julie and Cliff look at each other as Julie shakes her head and tells Cliff. "Must you be so needy?"

The next day Jack arrives in San Francisco and Sarah meets him at the airport. As soon as they see each other they run toward one another and embrace. Jack is wearing a red and white trucker hat that says "I heart San Francisco" on it. He never enjoyed California, but if he was going to be here, he would try to act excited for Sarah.

"Ok, are you ready to do all the touristy stuff like Alcatraz, Golden Gate Bridge, China Town, eat clam chowder, and whatever those Asian tourists do? We can just follow one of their buses. Wow, let's get started!"

"Wow, calm down sailor. First of all, don't be racist. Second, don't you want to slow down? You just got off a two-hour flight; don't you want to go to the hotel first? And how are you, Jack? I am doing great. Thanks for asking."

"First of all, slow down tiger. I know it's been months, but I want to spend quality time with you. We got all night to catch up physically, and also, you're right. I'm sorry. I'm just so excited to see you and don't want to waste a second."

Jack kisses Sarah, and she smiles as he holds her in his arms. He's missed her scent. She smells of sweet berries, and for the moment it didn't matter where they were, he would go to hell and back for the girl he held in his arms. She fit perfectly. He forgot how right it felt.

"Okay, what are we waiting for, slowpoke? Let's get going; this city isn't going to tour itself!" Sarah gleefully teases.

They spend the day enjoying all that San Francisco has to offer including eating clam chowder and visiting Alcatraz. Sarah stops Jack from following an Asian couple in Chinatown. They enjoy each other's company and it's like nothing has changed. After they visit Sarah's university, their last stop is the Golden Gate Bridge. By then, it's nightfall and the buildings are lit up. Jack and Sarah sit on a rock enjoying the view.

"Jack, isn't it beautiful? I know it's cheesy, but it feels like home, you know."

Jack keeps looking in the distance. "Yeah, but it's not your home. Salt Lake is. San Francisco is great, but it's not home," he says without thinking.

"Home is where you make it. Jack, let's talk hypotheticals. What if I want to live here when I'm done with school? Would you come down? I know you got your masters so you can get a job at a clinic here and maybe take breaks. My career will support the both of us. We can travel for my new career. When this all happens, would you be able to do this for me, Jack?"

"Hypothetically, if that were to happen, I guess I could move down here, but Sarah, let's be real. Art is not an actual career. When you're done having your fun down here, you will come home to me. You know you probably won't do anything with art, right?"

Sarah is furious as she jumps up and stands right in front of Jack. He does not know why she's so angry. He reaches out to comfort her but she just rejects his advances.

"Art is not a career! What the fuck is that supposed to mean? Why do you think I traveled all this way to go to a prestigious art school? As a hobby? No, this is my dream, Jack! I came here to fulfill that dream and who the fuck do you think you are to belittle my dreams! I'm sorry I don't have one of your fancy degrees, Jack. Art is my life. I didn't insult you when you were peddling drugs to rich doctors in a soulless, life-sucking job. You did not mind doing that because you are so insecure with yourself that you had to make lots of money to even feel something!"

Jack, now getting upset, loses all sense of reason, and stubbornly stands his ground. "I'm sorry I live in the real world where people have to get actual careers so they can put food on their plates and a fucking roof over their heads."

"Oh, look at me. I'm Mr. Has My Life Together. I know better than everyone, so everyone should just bow down to me and bend to my will!"

"You're being a child!"

"I'd rather be a child with dreams than a robot that crushes them!"

"You don't understand. I'm just being realistic. You know as well as anyone that trying to be a successful artist in this world is like playing Russian roulette with five bullets; it's practically career suicide."

"No! You don't understand. This has been my dream since I was a little girl. I could have been anything I wanted, but what I wanted to do was be an artist traveling the world to show the world there is beauty in this godforsaken place. Jack, I know how risky this is, but I don't care because this is my dream. A long time ago you said to me I look at this world with a pair of rose-colored goggles, but I never did. I realized that this world is filthy and unpleasant, not because I lived a tough life like you, but I learned from a young age. I know my sister told you about when I was a little girl, how I disappeared for hours, just for my family to find me admiring my neighbor's rose bush. What she didn't tell you was the reason I was there for hours. Nobody knew the real reason. I didn't tell anyone, even my sister." Sarah pauses for a beat. "It was because I had pricked my finger on one of the thorns and I was too ashamed to tell anyone. I pricked myself because it was beautiful and I had to have it. Life is like that rosebush, and I know that, but I don't want to be the thorn. I want to be the rose. It's the beautiful things people want, not the painful parts, but in life we get both. We can't have the beauty without the pain. And if I can provide just a slight bit more beauty to the world, then I will do everything in my power to provide that!"

"I know this is your dream. I won't impede that."

Sarah starts to tear up. "You're right. You won't get in the way because we are breaking up." This is the one thing he did not want to hear, not from her, especially not from her. She's his world, but those four words tore it apart.

"We can work this out. Just because I said—"

"No, it's not that. You told me from the very beginning that you never believed in me, not with words, but with the way you acted. You never once acknowledged my art dream. Sure, you said all the things I wanted to hear because you loved me. You always know the right things to say. Deep down I always knew you thought my dream was fruitless, but you finally said the thing I always feared you'd say to me, but that's fine because I believe in myself. Jack, I love you but no matter what you say from now on will not be true because in your heart you could never understand."

"Sarah!"

"I hope you get everything you want and one day you can see that it's okay to dream."

Jack starts to tear up as he stands at a complete loss for words. He's out of options. He has no counter argument and he cannot muster a single thought. For the first time in his life his mind is blank. There's no clever retort. He is overcome with sadness and confusion. He stands there frozen like the first time they had met but this time is different. Instead of love at first sight, it feels like all the love he ever had has been violently ripped out of his chest as he clenches his heart, which feels like it has gained a hundred pounds in an instant, tightening in his chest. His throat has a lump that causes a quiver in his lip. It's like he just swallowed a bag of marbles. Sarah hugs him and kisses his cheek as she disappears, leaving Jack motionless.

28

— . —

BACKWARD WALKING

Love is a fleeting thing. One moment you feel you are on top of the world, the next you are plummeting down in a deep pit of sorrow. For Jack, he thought he found true undying love but he lost it in an instant. From the moment Sarah left to the moment he got home, he kept replaying that night in his head over and over. All he sees is Sarah walking away. She gets smaller and smaller as she disappears into the distance.

That night Jack cried himself to sleep. He flew out of California the next day, dropping off chocolates at the salon, not wanting to see her friends. He spent the first week in silence, and the first month engulfing himself with more work than ever. On the last day of that month after the breakup, he finds himself alone at a bar, swirling a glass of brown liquid sitting in silence and deep in thought. Suddenly an attractive redhead sits next to him and starts a conversation.

"Long day in the office?"

"Long month."

"Oh really, where do you work?"

"Sales."

"Wow, you are a man of very few words, aren't you?"

"I guess."

"Well then, my name is Rebecca. I work in retail, not my dream. I want to be a nurse, thanks for asking."

Jack grabs Rebecca softly by the face and kisses her to shut her up. "Listen, I do not care to get to know you, and I will not bother to tell you about myself because I will not see you after tomorrow morning. You are extremely attractive and I am incredibly sad and just tipsy enough to make a terrible decision. So I am going to pay for our drinks. You will say goodbye to your friends that dared you to talk to the man sitting alone at the bar. Then we will go back to my place where I will fuck your brains out. I just ordered an Uber. We've got five minutes. Let's go."

Rebecca gazes at Jack with a look of shock and excitement. "Okay!"

29

TAKE US AWAY REGINALD

<u>One week after the breakup</u>

Ruth bursts through Big Mama's doors. "Close up early. We are going to San Francisco," Ruth says, getting the attention of Julie, Cliff, and the clients they were working on.

"Cliff, I have no time to deal with Ruth's antics Get rid of her!" Julie sighs.

"Hi, Ruth. How are you? Oh, me? I'm fine, thanks for asking. That's how regular people greet each other. Try it sometime," Cliff says as he focuses on his client's hair. "As you can see, crazy lady, we are busy."

"I have no time for your sass boy! Or even an obligatory exchange of greetings that we have all shared before. The point is my sister is in pain, and she needs me. And since I hate traveling alone, I thought I'd drag you two along with me because she likes you guys or something like that." Ruth says as she gestures to the door. "Now just buzz Karen and Susan's hair and lock the doors behind you!"

"Ruth, we love Sarah as much as you because we are her best friends! But we own this place and we have responsibilities. We can't just drop everything and go to Sarah every time she breaks up with some boy," Cliff says as he reassures his customer.

"Some boy! Do you hear yourself? This was Sarah's first true love. She was there for me when I ended things with Ralph, who almost fathered my child. Cliff, I know you've experienced true love. Even Julie has her reflection."

"Watch it, blondie!" Julie barks. "Sarah's a big girl who has broken up with dozens of men, in fact, she's the expert at breaking men's hearts. And Sarah didn't have any pregnancy scares because she's not as empty-minded and irrational as you are."

"Ouch, Tin Man called, and he wants his empty void where a heart should be back. Come on, if you come with me, I'll ignore all the mean things you say to me," Ruth begs, getting down on her knees.

"You never think things through. Let's say we came with you. We would have to cancel all our appointments for the next two days. Not to mention it takes twelve hours to drive from here to San Francisco. And that is not accounting for rest stops, food, and gas. Not all of us are cartoon characters like you. We can't just travel on a whim!" Julie says, finishing her client's haircut.

Ruth grows silent for a moment. She knows it's an impossible task, but she has to persevere. These were Sarah's best friends; she listens to them. Ruth used to get jealous when the three grew closer. She and Sarah had been attached at the hip till she went to college, and it's because of these two that she has become a strong and independent woman. She just sits there until they both finish with their customers, glaring at them until Cliff's customer leaves. She runs to the doors and locks them behind her. "Ha, now you're not working. Let's go!"

"Dammit, you can't just impede a business like that. Even if everything is paid for, we don't even have a change of clothes!" Julie says, rolling her eyes.

"Easy, wear my clothes, and I'll pay. We'll even take Reginald," Ruth says.

"Regi—oh, that God awful red Elantra you gave a boy's name to? Your clothes won't fit either of us. Cliff is a thousand feet tall and you're dreaming if you think those size zero jeans are fitting over my voluptuous ass," Julie hisses

"Actually, I think I can rock a crop. She's got cute tops." Cliff mimes wearing one of Ruth's tops.

"Idiots, the both of you!" Julie says, crossing her arms.

"The both- Cliff are you coming?" Ruth queries excitedly.

"Yeah, I guess I'll come. We can buy new outfits in San Fran. They have better malls anyway, and you had me at true love. My first true love was Ben in high school, he came out for me."

"Yippee! Now I won't be alone! All right, let's go!" Ruth says, heading toward the door.

"Wait!" Julie says reluctantly. "I'll come," Julie says as both look at her in shock. "Pick your jaws up off the ground. If you two are going you need a proper adult to watch you, and I care about Sarah too. My first love, their name was Jamie."

"Also, if we are going to San Francisco, we need to stop by Ghirardelli's for ice cream." Cliff locks the doors behind them.

"Don't be an idiot, Cliff," Ruth says with a straight face. "Of course, we are going to Ghirardelli. I'm not insane!" Smiling, she then skips to her car and the two follow her to Reginald.

The trip goes by quickly. They all arrive at Sarah's apartment and see the light on in her bedroom window, so they barge into her apartment. Her room is covered in hundreds of canvases covered with attempts of what looks like the same painting--a rosebush. Sarah's obviously in some kind of awful mindset. She's chewing on her paintbrush, observing what looks like attempt number three hundred and nine. Ruth sneaks up behind her but then walks in front of the painting since Sarah doesn't even notice that they entered her apartment. Sarah stares forward in a hyper focus that's only interrupted by her painting a red splotch on Ruth's face. "Dammit Ruthie, you're not a canvas!" Sarah screams.

"Speak for yourself. This body was made to be turned into art," Ruth says, striking a pose.

"Ruthie! I have no time for your childish antics. I have to finish getting this piece just right or it won't be displayed in the gala next month." Sarah looks around the room and notices Cliff and Julie standing behind her snickering at Ruth. "And why the hell did you drag these two into whatever coup you dreamed up to ruin my life!"

"Hi, it's nice to see you too!" Cliff exclaims.

Julie storms up to Sarah and lifts her up by her shirt, looking down briefly. "Victoria, I know your secret," she says before refocusing on Sarah's face. "Listen here, missy. We didn't travel hundreds of miles in your sister's crappy car just for you to be a little bitch. So, you're going to sit here silent and let us comfort you dammit!" Julie says as she throws Sarah onto her bed.

"You're here to comfort me? But I don't need comforting. I'm fine, no need for my two knucklehead friends and eccentric sister to come and comfort me. I'm fine!" she says, grabbing her shirt and clenching it to her chest.

"Look around, Sarah. Three hundred of the same painting does not say fine. You're blocked. It's not good. You need to let your emotions flow," Ruth says, navigating through various canvases.

"They are not the same painting." Sarah points to a random painting. "That one, the thorns are more obtuse than acute, that one had too much yellow in the bush, and that one, oh that one, the colors blended together to make ugly brown splurges randomly throughout." Sarah picks up another painting. "And this one—guys, I'm fine."

"Say it one more time. We will believe you." Cliff sits on one side of Sarah.

"I'm...why are you guys here?" Sarah says as she lays her head on Cliff's shoulder.

"We're here because we're worried about you, dumbass!" Julie says as she sits on the other side of Sarah, rubbing her back.

Ruth looks at Sarah as she looks back. She knows she is thanking her, but she still has to say things out loud so the others can understand. "Sarah, we love you. I know it hurts, but we need to talk about this so you can get to a clearer mindset," Ruth says as she takes her hands.

"The woman takes one psychology class, now she's Dr. Guy. I don't want to talk about it." Sarah lets go of Ruth's hands.

"Honey, we know it's painful but we are here so you can release your pain," Cliff says, kissing her head.

Ruth just stares at Sarah with an intimidating gaze.

"Shut up. I can't talk about it!"

"Why not?" Ruth says, baiting Sarah.

"Because if I even think of him, I will spiral into misery. Or worse, I'll call him up and he will forgive me." Tears roll down Sarah's redden cheeks. "I can't go down that rabbit hole because it's more than just a hole. It's a pit, an endless pit. If I think for one second that leaving him was the wrong choice, then not only am I a fool, but I'm also a quitter." Sarah hyperventilates but catches her composure. "He doesn't believe I can achieve my dream, but I have more than one dream. The first was to become stupidly successful with my art, the second was to spend the rest of my life with him. In that order. He would rather just skip ahead to two, but I've loved art a lot longer than him." Sarah stands up, pacing. "Sometimes I think, what if I were to give up on my dream? What does that make me? It makes me scum." Sarah looks at her friend's concern. "I also wonder if being scum won't be so bad. Ninety percent of people give up on their dreams all the time. That's not me though. I love him, yes, but I need to do this without him. If I even think of him, I lose focus on my dream, and my art." Sarah pauses, looking around her at the art. "If I lose focus for even a moment of weakness, I can't perform properly. If I can't perform, then I flunk out of my dream college. If I flunk out, then I truly give up on my dream. And if I have no more dreams, then I'm worse than scum."

Sarah sits back down on her bed and buries her head in her hands, weeping uncontrollably. But Julie and Cliff embrace her while Ruth embraces the three, taking most of Sara's tears. "Guys, I'm a mess," Sarah whimpers, soaking Ruth's shirt in her tears. All four continue to embrace, being there to support Sarah.

30

BECOMING SIGMUND

The next morning, Tim stumbles out of his bedroom, not noticing the half-naked girl in his kitchen as he starts his lecture. "Jack, I know you are lonely, but can you use headphones when listening to your porn like us normal people? I could hear moaning all the way in my room, which is quite the feat considering the distance between our rooms!"

Rebecca snickers as she takes a drink from a coffee mug.

Tim suddenly notices the girl in the kitchen. He's not surprised but has not walked in on a half-naked girl since Jack saw Sarah regularly. Keeping his cool, he switches to his calm, flirty voice.

"Oh, hey I did not notice you. I'm Tim, and I don't watch porn. That's just Jack—I was making a point—but now I know what the voices were."

Rebecca laughs into her coffee mug. "Don't worry, and I'm sorry I did not know he had a roommate. This place doesn't even look lived in. It's quite impressive."

"Not to brag too much, but I am a neat freak and Jack is clean, so we mesh pretty well. Speaking of Jack, where did he go?"

"Oh, he is already gone. I woke up with a note that told me to make myself coffee and that it was okay to shower here. I woke up to my clothes folded nicely on a chair. The note also said he was getting breakfast. You know, for a guy like Jack, I'm surprised he is so considerate. In fact, he may be the most considerate man I've ever slept with. This includes ex-boyfriends!"

"Yea, he is great. I have to ask. You're a beautiful woman. What is it about Jack that is like a magnet for gorgeous girls?"

"That's a simple answer. It is the fact that he just doesn't care."

"I thought girls like a guy that cares?"

"Yes, we look for that in a boyfriend, sure, but not in someone who we just want to sleep with."

"Explain yourself. I do not understand."

"So many guys in my life bend over backward just to impress me. I have seen him at the same bar at that the same time for a month and he did not even show any interest. Even when I talked to him, I barely got two-word answers. He was distant and that is a perfect person to just sleep with because we know we won't break his heart."

"Okay, I get it. I'll have to try that."

"It won't work." Rebecca says with a chuckle.

"Why not?" Tim says defensively.

"You reek of someone who cares; it would not work."

Jack walks in carrying coffees and a few bags. As he enters, Rebecca perks up as he announces.

"Honey, I'm home!" Jack puts down his things, handing Tim a coffee and excuses the situation. "Good morning, Tim, I see you have already met Rebecca, and she is half-naked. Didn't you get my note you can shower here?"

Rebecca grabs Jack's arm and rubs her finger on his chest. "I took a shower. I just thought I'd wear one of your shirts instead of my street clothes just for a bit."

Tim interjects before Jack could debate. "Jack, it's fine. Sarah used to come in wearing a lot less than one of your shirts."

"Who's Sarah?" Rebecca helps herself to some fruit. Jack freezes and Tim covers his mouth realizing what he just said.

"Finish breakfast, get dressed, and please leave. I have plans for today. You will be bored if you stuck around. Thanks for last night. I'll see you around."

Jack grabs his guitar and leaves as Rebecca calls out, "Okay, call me!"

Tim gapes at Rebecca with confusion and pity, and in an inquiring tone he states, "Really?"

Jack runs up the stairs to the roof with his guitar. After Rebeca gets dressed and Tim shoos her out the door, he runs after Jack to make sure he doesn't do anything too rash. When he gets to the roof he hears Jack playing his guitar. This is a shock because he never really knew Jack could actually play. It's shockingly decent as Jack plays a rendition of Streets. Tim listens from a distance as Jack sings.

"Sitting on the roof.

Looking for the living proof

That I am still alive

That my heart still beats

And I find the relief.

And the will to sur-vive..."

Jack then stops, stares at his guitar intently, grips it tightly in his hand as he tears up. He then stands up and raises his guitar over his head like he was wielding an ax to chop wood. He lets out a scream, then suddenly he violently smashes the guitar against the ground as he is pounding what remains of the neck of the guitar on the ground. Tim walks up and stops Jack by grabbing his shoulders and throwing the splintered wood with strings curling up wildly out of the way. Once Jack seems calm enough to talk, Tim lets go as he faces the flustered Jack.

"Whoa, buddy. What did that guitar do to you?"

"I didn't even want a guitar. I just got it because I thought it would be a hobby to pick up girls, but it doesn't. It can't even keep any girls that are worth having around."

"Okay, I get it, it's a terrible investment. You should have smashed it a long time ago."

"But I loved it, then it decided to move to California, explore itself, become an artist, and move to Europe. It broke my heart way before I shattered it!"

"Oh, we shifted to obvious metaphors now and no longer care about the guitar. Listen, buddy, it's been a month. I know it may seem to be okay to sleep with random redheads and smash acoustic guitars, but you need to talk to someone. Let me know and until then we will not mention you know who again."

"I don't want to talk about it again!" Jack gets up and heads toward the exit. He turns around and addresses Tim.

"And Tim, thanks. I appreciate you. I just need to figure things out by myself right now. Thanks for being a friend."

Tim has never seen Jack in such a funk. The next few months are hard for Jack as he transitions from his random women phase to his mourning period to his moping around phase of the breakup. He didn't even laugh at Monty Python, which is a crime in Tim's book. He hasn't talked to Tim much after breaking the guitar. Jack walks out of his room like a zombie and plops himself on the couch. Tonight it seems different. Did Jack finally want to talk? Tim grabs a chair and sits next to Jack.

"Tim, what's wrong with me?" Jack relents.

"Nothing," Tim states while he crosses his legs, smoking a pretend pipe. "Tell me, my boy, what makes you feel this way? Is it a lack of sex?" he relays in a terrible German accent.

"No, Sigmund, it's a lack of connection!" Jack barks.

"All right, sorry," Tim states in his normal voice. "How can I help, buddy?"

"Tim, have you ever been in love?"

Tim was in shock. In the two years he has known him, he had never asked about his past relations. Maybe that's because Jack assumed Tim's inexperience is the reason he never asks. Tim remains fine with Jack never asking about his love life; most people underestimate him. Part of him is happy Jack finally asked. So joyfully he responds, "Actually, I have!" Tim leans closer to Jack, "Her name was Angela. We dated for the four years I was in college." Tim sits up and remembers how she made him feel. "She was perfect. She liked action movies and she had an incredible laugh; and most importantly, she loved me for me."

Jack sits up. "What happened?"

"One day she just left. I remember like it was yesterday. We had a date planned for that night, but she never showed up." Tim swallows the lump in his throat. "I just sat there in the rain waiting for a girl who was never going to show up."

"I'm sorry to hear that man. Why would she do such a terrible thing?"

"I found out years later it was because she had met someone from her past. He was twice her age. They had a beautiful baby boy together. She was too scared to tell me, something about how I wouldn't understand." Tim stands. "Jack, you're not the only one who has experienced heartbreak. It happens to everyone at some point."

Jack stands. "Tim, I never knew."

"You never asked," Tim says, smiling sheepishly.

"You know you're a lot wiser than you appear."

"Thanks, can you tell my mom?"

"Yeah, I'll tell her when I see her tonight." Jack winks. This is the first joke he's told in months.

"Oh, you have jokes now!" Tim puts Jack in a headlock. "Jokes on you. My mom only dates tall men."

Both laugh as they wrestle for a bit. From that time on, his relationship with Jack was better.

31

_— • —_

WHAT IS SMASH ALL TRULY ABOUT?

<u>Eleven months later</u>

Jack is sitting in his office typing on his computer, fidgeting with a pen in his fingers as his knee shakes up and down. He grabs his side bag and marches himself to his boss's office, shocking Mr. Johnson to attention.

"Jack, what is this about?" Mr. Johnson says, in bewilderment.

"Mr. Johnson, I quit!"

"Whoa, settle down Jack, there is a procedure to this. We need to look for a replacement, and you need to put in two weeks, and put in the proper paperwork through the right channels."

"With all due respect sir, I will do none of that shit. Instead this is what's going to happen. I am going to walk out that door right now because I already clocked out. In two weeks, I will get my final check in the mail that will include the vacation pay I acquired this year. Tim will take my position because I have been preparing him for over a year now. I appreciate the opportunity and wish you luck with the future of this company."

"May I ask why you are doing this?" Mr. Johnson says.

"Sir, I've been in a rut for years. I've stayed doing this job that I hate for money that I hardly spend. And this whole time I've ignored my dream. I want to help people and not by selling drugs."

"It looks like you give me no choice. Okay. Good luck Jack. You were one hell of an employee. We are going to miss having you around, but I understand a man's gotta do what a man's gotta do." Mr. Johnson stands. "I know that you probably don't want it, but by this time tomorrow you will have my letter of recommendation for any job you desire."

"Thank you, sir."

Jack leaves the office and walks to City Creek Park where he loves to go to. He stands on the bridge, looking at the beautiful little creek that runs through the park. Jack looks up and sees a man scribbling on an overly used notebook. At first Jack doesn't think of it, but then upon a second glance he realizes he knows who this has to be. He runs up to the bench and inquires.

"Are you Ken Winters, the author of Smash Ball?"

"Yes, but I wrote more than just Smash Ball. I also wrote Idiots in Love; you know, the one that actually became a movie. It won an award for best costume design, several Razzies, and is still available for purchase, but no one cares about that. All anyone ever wants to know is about Smash Ball; when is the movie coming out, did you get the Rock to play Coach Grizzlies? The answers are soon enough and I'm talking with him; he's a busy guy."

"Okay, but I need to know- Ask, can I?" Jack gestures to the spot next to Ken,

"Yes, please have a seat. Sorry I blew up. When you only have one successful book, I try to push the others."

"Not a problem. I love your books, even the first two with terrible grammar, but I have a question about Smash Ball."

"Very well, shoot."

"Okay, what is it about? I mean, what is the specific genre? Some people think it is a sports novel, while others think it is a romance. I say it's a comprehensive satire and look at the human race's need for increased violence."

"Wow, how smart do you think I am? Never mind. It's none of the above. What I wrote is science fiction. That is the genre I categorized it under, no subcategories, no secret genre with clues hidden in the subtext. People think I'm a lot smarter than I actually am. But as for what the message I am trying to convey in Smash Ball, that is simple, it is about teamwork. Zack starts off his hero's journey as a self-centered athlete with massive potential that would have led to nothing if he would not have met the people in his life. As soon as he meets his team, he can complete his journey. The reason I had Zack compete in a team sport is because the team needed each other to win. In life, we do nothing alone; even if you are talented or smart, we can only do so much by ourselves. No hero's journey is complete without a dedicated team behind them. Even Odysseus, who is the original hero, received help along his hero's journey. So, it's about teamwork. It's that simple."

"So, what you're saying is that even you didn't do it by yourself?"

"You're damn right, I did not do it by myself. I have my publisher and several angels of editors because I'm not college educated. They do a lot of work, and support of friends and family to spread the word."

"Is it okay if I ask you a personal question?" Jack queries eagerly.

"Sure, what is it?" Ken says hesitantly.

"I just quit my job, and I started applying for my dream job, something I should have done six years ago, but that is beside the point. I followed my dream after dating this wonderful girl, but she has been out of my life for a while, and I don't know if I did the right thing, like if I'm doing it for myself or am doing it because I was with her."

"This girl, did you love her?"

"Yes, I haven't been in love with anyone else. I thought I was before her, but that wasn't love. In fact, I don't know how to handle things without her."

"You have to. I know it hurts, but in the end no girl wants to be with an incomplete man. If you cannot move forward without her, you will never have her."

"How do you know so much about relationships?" Jack says raising an eyebrow.

"Boy, I started writing nothing but romance, so I know a thing or two about it. At the end of the day, love is simple. When two people love each other, it just works," Ken says with such confidence, even if it wasn't true, Jack would still believe it.

"If love is so easy, why does it hurt so much?"

"You know that song by Poison, 'Every Rose Has Its Thorn?' Love is like a rose, beautiful, simple, and a bit cliché; but there are thorns that get in our way, thorns like insecurities, doubts, someone saying something they can't take back. Just because there are thorns does not change the fact that they are still beautiful."

"Funny. This girl said something remarkably similar."

"Then she is smart and sounds like a keeper. Honestly, I just have roses on my mind because I just bought a painting called 'Rose Bush' from this up-and-coming artist. It's absolutely breathtaking."

Jack has a realization but keeps it to himself. "Do you think I can do this without her?" Jack says, ignoring the inkling to ask about the artist.

"It doesn't matter what I think. The important thing is for you to follow your dream, no matter what. You know many people don't know this, but Idiots in Love was not my first book."

"Yea, it was Unplugged, a short story with the most misleading title. What's your point?"

"Unplugged was my first published book, the first full-length novel was a little-known book called The Ceiling. It was a romance about two people who are truly in love despite flaws and situations."

"You just described half of all romance novels that exist. Replace situations with vampires, and you have the other half."

"My point is The Ceiling was my magnum opus. I spent years researching and writing it, but it gained no traction. It was not until I wrote Smash Ball that I became recognized and famous. I do not regret writing The Ceiling because I loved every second. If I would have given up on writing because my first book failed, I would have never written Smash Ball, and I'd probably still be peddling dresses half off."

"Okay then, how will I know I'm doing the right thing with my life?"

"You just will. It is like a moment of clarity. Just a tip, but clarity is easily achieved when you clear your mind of distractions. Now I'm writing my next book and I need some time to think," Ken says, making a shooing motion with his hand.

Jack gets up, shaking the author's hand. "Thank you so much, sir. One more thing. Can you sign my copy of Smash Ball? I keep it with me to look smart."

Jack pulls out a pen and the book handing it to Ken, who signs it, pulls out a different book and tells Jack, "Here you go. Take this. It's a copy of The Ceiling. You really should read it. I think it will help with your girl."

Jack looks at Ken in bewilderment, accepting the book with a bow. He thanks him and walks away in shock at what just occurred.

32

HEAD JACKASS

"I have a master's in psychology. I spent six years in sales where I would convince doctors and pharmacies to buy drugs they did not need. The last two years, I was building up the sales team, working with more people on a personal level. I know it's not the same correlation but I believe my ability to connect with people could be an enormous asset to this job," Jack recites to the man in scrubs sitting right across from him.

"Okay then, Mr. Salinger, what makes you think you are the right fit for the job? Yes, your credentials are great, and your old boss gave you a glowing letter of recommendation. But why do you want to be our rehabilitation specialist?"

"Sir, if I may speak bluntly. I have been a selfish jackass my whole life. Excuse my language, but it's the truth. I thought it was about time I gave back a little, and besides, ever since I was a child, I wanted to do this. It was my only dream. I know it may seem odd, but I wanted to help people starting with the heart and mind, the rest will follow."

"The point of rehab is to have selfish jackasses to work as a team, to create new opportunities in their life, so I think our team could use a former jackass as their fearless leader. Also, you have a master's in psychology, and years of excellent leadership experience, which is enough to qualify alone. The passion helps though. Congratulations Jack, you got the job. When can you start?"

"Sir, I could start tomorrow if you wanted me to."

"How does Monday at nine sound?"

"Sounds good."

The doctor stands up, shakes Jack's hand.

Later that day, Jack bursts into his apartment to find Tim watching television. "Honey, I'm home!"

"Hey, Jack, how'd it go?"

"I got the job. I start next week."

"Well, that is fantastic. What are you going to be doing again, talking with crazy people?"

"No, I am going to make sure people in rehabilitation are good enough to go back into society. Let's go to the roof. It's a beautiful day. I'd hate to waste it."

Jack and Tim make their way to the roof as they joke around. When they get there they see a small blonde woman standing on the roof looking at the view with her back facing the two men. Jack stands still for a moment and wonders if this is really happening. Then in a rash moment he runs to the girl, with Tim trailing behind him. As he reaches her, he exclaims.

"Sarah!"

The girl turns around in surprise at what has just happened, and Jack steps back, his face filling with regret. He realizes this blonde woman he had just assaulted is not Sarah. The girl chuckles and introduces herself, consoling Jack. The girl is a petite woman who stands at an impressive four-foot-eleven. She's wearing distressed denim jeans, a baby blue sweater and wears light makeup, bringing out her lips and her bright green eyes. She has a smile that seems like a permanent fixture on her face. Her presence is warm and nurturing. She consoles the flabbergasted Jack.

"I'm sorry, my name is Stephanie, not Sarah. I wish I could say this is the first time someone has mistaken me for someone else. One of those faces, I guess; at least you didn't try to kiss me." She chuckles awkwardly.

Jack backs away, bowing his head as he justifies himself. "I'm sorry I got—well, I thought... my name is Jack. I should go, um. This is Tim. He's a great guy. You guys should talk."

Jack pushes Tim in front of him and leaves back the way he came, smiling to himself, knowing he did the right thing, but not how yet. Tim shakes the girl's hand nervously.

33

SHE'S PERFECT

"So, who is Sarah?"

Tim rubs his head nervously as he says the first thing he could utter. "A girl Jack met in the same spot you are standing in right now."

"Oh, really, does he meet a lot of girls here?"

"Surprisingly, yes. Do you want to talk to him? Normally girls are only interested in him. I'll go get him."

Tim walks away as Stephanie grabs his arm, stopping him.

"Don't, he's not my type, anyway."

Tim turns around and smiles proudly.

"Oh really, why is that?"

"He is obviously hung up on an ex. I've been the girl after the one and I don't want to do that again. Besides, I'm done dating jerks. I am ready for a nice guy."

"Well, in that case, I am a nice guy. Can I buy you flowers or open the door of your car or carriage?"

"Ha, sure, while you're at it, could you defend my honor, pull out my chair, and put your coat over puddles?"

"Why, of course, I can do all that and so much more."

Both laugh and look each other in the eyes before sharing hours of incredible conversation. Tim comes down to the apartment with a huge smile on his face. As he barges into the apartment, Jack peeks from the book that he's reading as he asks, "So, how'd it go?"

"Amazing, man, we talked for like a long time. She's so funny and actually listens when I talk. I know that it's early, but she may be the one!"

"Wow, you have her at Neo status! Should I be worried?"

"Only if this number is fake." Tim pulls out his phone to show Jack, and Jack smiles as he sits up.

"Wow, congratulations, man! I knew you could do it."

"Wait, you knew, how?"

"I just did."

"Wait, you did this on purpose, didn't you?" Tim says in shock. Jack nods and Tim smiles and embraces Jack. "Thank you!"

A few days later, Tim starts to frantically go over a list while Jack lies on the couch.

"Looking great. Polo shows that I like to dress nice but I'm not trying too hard, deodorant as I sniff my pit—smells ok, so yes, I put on a couple of squirts of cologne."

Tim squirts the bottle on the back of his neck and his wrist before putting on his watch. He looks at Jack. "Am I forgetting anything?" Without looking up from his book, Jack recites a list of things.

"Wallet, keys, the confidence to know that this is just a date and if it's meant to be, things will go just right."

Tim checks his pockets as he responds, "Yes, yes, and, hey!"

"Just looking out for you, brother."

"Okay, respect."

Tim checks his pocket one more time, then leaves Jack as they wave goodbye to one another.

Tim walks down the hall to the elevator expecting the worst. Normally, when a woman looks at him it's out of pity or disgust, but Stephanie's different. She has a warm personality that is at odds with indifferent opinions. He couldn't help but wonder if it was all just an act and she would be like all the other girls and just pass him up without a second thought. Before reaching the lobby, Tim closes his eyes and takes a deep breath. As the doors open, he sees Stephanie standing there in a sundress with a jean jacket clutched in her hand as she sways back and forth admiring the giant painting of a potted flower. Tim walks up, stands right beside her, but she doesn't notice his presence.

"Ah, I love this piece, a painting derived from the style of every other art in every other lobby. It's like it was painted by a robot."

Stephanie stays forward facing, still not acknowledging Tim. "Actually, my cousin painted this!" Tim stumbles as he apologizes, she continues in a less serious tone. "As a matter of fact, he is part robot, his first words were..." She moves in a fake robot gesture and continues in a robot voice, "Beep boop, system booting!"

They both laugh, as this is the beginning of the best first date either of them has ever been on. The conversation flows like they have known each other for their whole lives; they laugh and enjoy each other's company. Tim often acts rash and quirky; he is not afraid to be himself, especially with Stephanie. Despite her petite stature, Stephanie carries with her a giant personality. She is very excitable and would keep her spirits up when any normal human being would run out of energy, and she laughs at all of Tim's terrible jokes. They both love movies so they would talk about their shared interest. They were the couple that would wear couples costumes every year, and when they were in the room, you knew you were in the presence of a power couple. In short, they were a perfect match.

34

GIVING A WEDDING TOAST

Jack is dressed in a button-down shirt, khakis, a tie, a cardigan, and brown shoes holding a notebook as he sits in a circle of men and women dressed in gray scrubs and slippers in a professionally landscaped garden. Jack stands up and addresses the group. "All right guys, that's a wrap. I will see you all at the same time and place next week."

The group disperses as Jack leaves the center and answers his ringing phone.

"Hey, Tim. Don't worry, I got the spot reserved and I am picking up the balloons right now. Okay, breathe, it will go great. You two are perfect. Do you have everything you need? Okay, good. Do you have the ring? All right, you have everything you need. See you soon. Okay, bye."

—ell—

Later that night, Jack, Tim, and Stephanie are walking in a beautiful garden area alone. Stephanie and Tim are holding hands and Stephanie asks Tim, "I'm glad you have brought me to one of my favorite places in Salt Lake, but why is Jack with us?"

Tim glares at Jack. Jack ponders how he can recover.

"You see, babe... you know... uh, that he is, uh—is lonely. Yeah, that's it. Jack has been so lonely lately I thought I'd just bring him along," Tim states, rubbing the back of his neck.

Stephanie stares at Jack, whose expression does not change because he's pretending not to pay attention to the couple. "He doesn't look that lonely."

"You know us men, we don't show our emotions."

"But you cried last night when we were watching Good Night Moon!"

Tim quickly shushes Stephanie.

"Jack doesn't wear his emotions on his sleeve like I do."

Stephanie buys it as they continue to the center of the garden that is decorated with balloons and has a band playing. Jack films the whole thing as Stephanie bursts with excitement and she exclaims, "Tim, what does this mean?"

Tim gets down on one knee and pulls out a velvet box revealing a ring with a sizable round cut diamond on top.

"Stephanie Bellows, will you marry me?"

Stephanie cries tears of joy as she squeals with excitement. "Yes, yes, I will marry you a thousand times, yes!"

Tim stands up and the two embrace and kiss. After he slips the ring on her finger, Jack slips away to leave the two to celebrate alone. The two were engaged for six months that had them stressed with all the planning and annoyed Jack with their inexhaustible dynamic, but they were just ready to spend their lives together.

Jack stands on the right side of Tim at the end of an aisle paved with red roses in a well-tailored suit with a pink boutonniere in his lapel. On his left stands Tim's two older brothers, Ezra, and David. Tim wears a bright white suit with a pink vest and a black oxford, eagerly awaiting the wedding march to be played. Stephanie, with a bright smile, glides down the aisle. Her bright yellow hair is braided in a princess braid. She wears a baby blue and silver necklace and a long, flowing white wedding dress that has to be held by her maid of honor. Tim's oldest sister, Bethany, wears a tasteful baby blue dress. Each step Stephanie takes reveals glimpses of her baby blue heels that change Stephanie's four-foot eleven stature to a slightly taller five-foot-one. Tim stands in awe as he marvels at the beauty of his soon-to-be wife. Her father hands Stephanie over to Tim, who gently grabs her hands as the officiant begins the ceremony.

After what seems like an hour of reading various bible verses and introductions, the couple maintains focus on each other's eyes, holding strong as they grasp each other's hand anxiously waiting for their part to speak. The officiant finally gets to the part they have been waiting for.

"Do you, Timothy Smith, take this woman to be your wife, to have and to hold from this day forward for better, for worse, for richer, for poorer, in sickness and in health, to love and to cherish until death do you part?"

Tim nods. "I do!"

The officiant then turns to Stephanie. "Do you, Stephanie Bellows, take this man to be your husband, to have and to hold from this day forward for better, for worse, for richer, for poorer, in sickness, and in health to love and to cherish until death do you part?"

Stephanie nods, holding back tears of excitement. "I do!"

The officiant smiles. "By the power vested in me, by the state of Utah, I now pronounce you husband and wife. You may now kiss the bride."

Tim leans in and kisses Stephanie as the crowd cheers.

Later that night, Jack taps his champagne glass gently, getting the crowd's attention as he toasts.

"Ladies and gentlemen, this would be the first time I'm giving a toast at a wedding that I was actually invited to give."

The audience laughs, and Jack waits for them to calm down before continuing. "I met Tim a little over four years ago. He was the first person I met in Utah. When I first met him, I had the thought I'm sure many of you thought when you first met Tim. I thought he was a little awkward and that he was a massive goober."

The crowd laughs.

Tim's eyes widen at this realization, but he agrees after thinking about it for a beat.

Jack continues once the crowd settles down.

"But this little goober, despite my feelings at first, has grown on me. In fact, he has grown on me so much that I am honored to call him my best friend. Two years ago, I faced some terribly tough times, and Tim was there even when I did not want his help, but he helped me regardless. I am eternally grateful he was, and is, on my team now. Tim met Stephanie one and a half years ago and from the moment they met, I have never seen Tim as happy as he is when he is with you, Stephanie. Before he met you, he was a good man, but with you he is an even greater man. You bring out all his best qualities and the two of you are the perfect example of what love can become when properly nourished and cared for by a perfect team. Your love has the potential to become as perfect as perfect can be. Keep looking at each other the way you look at each other now. Keep loving each other the way you love each other now and never give up on one another. The two of you give me hope and inspire me daily. I love you and wish you an eternity of happiness. So, let's all raise a glass to the best couple I know--to Mr. And Ms. Timothy Smith, hear hear!"

The crowd raise their glasses and all at once shout, "Hear here!"

Jack remains standing for a moment as Tim and Stephanie look deep into each other's eyes. He smiles as he sits down. He did not get kicked out of this wedding.

———eee———

Later that night, Jack is dancing with a small girl who had asked him to dance. They are having an enjoyable time, when suddenly he feels a tap on his shoulder. He smells a hint of sweet berries as a familiar voice asks, "May I cut in?"

Jack peeks over his shoulder. "Sarah?" He doesn't know if she is real or if he is dreaming again.

Sarah nods as she reaches out her arms. Jack winks at Tim, who gives him a reassuring nod. He wraps his arm around her waist as she drapes her arms around his neck. They dance in silence for a moment. Sarah's eyes are just as bright and blue as always. Jack had forgotten how much they shine. Her smell is still just as intoxicating. *Fresh berries*. They both sway in silence until they start speaking at the same time.

"How ha—I mean—you look—wow!"

They both stop for a while to gather their thoughts until Jack gestures to Sarah to speak. She immediately blurts out, "You never wrote!"

Jack just smiles. "Sorry. I said that while we were still dating. I didn't think..."

"Exactly. I knew we weren't together, but that's no excuse," Sarah says.

"Okay, I'll write from now on. How about that? Do you still have the same address?"

"Yes, and my number is also the same."

"Good to know, how did you—I mean, why did you—well, you know."

"Tim got in touch with me. He told me it was important to him that I come to his wedding, so I, and I quote, 'don't feel too bad about him rejecting me'. I was hesitant at first, but I thought I might run into you, so here I am."

"Well, that little so and so."

They both dance in silence.

"Jack, I'm seeing someone," Sarah says hesitantly.

Jack has no reaction and just smiles as they dance in silence for a moment longer.

"Okay, when did this happen? I'm guessing he's another tall and handsome doctor type."

"Well, he's tall, but he's no doctor. Do you remember Jeremy? Well, it's him, but we didn't start dating till like four months ago after I returned from my second trip to Europe. Both were funded by some paintings I sold. My first painting was bought by an anonymous buyer who paid a lot for it. The piece was called 'Rose Bush'. A simple piece with wild green thorns and bleeding roses. It was hard, but I did it despite all the thorns that were in my path. Anyway, after we broke up, I honestly thought I would meet no one who I would ever feel the same way about. But he wore me down and I think I may love him. He's not you, sure, but he doesn't need to be you. He has his own thing going for him. He's smart, sure, but he's sweet and artistic, but most importantly I'm happy when I'm with him, but Jack, you know..."

Jack put a finger on Sarah's lips and smiles. "Sarah, you do not have to justify it for me; it's been over two years since we dated. I am just happy you found someone who makes you happy, and I don't care who that is. I will still write you and will say it's from your gay pen pal Phil so he doesn't get mad."

Both laugh until Sarah asks, "Jack, you seem different. Not in a bad way, but you look as if a huge burden has been lifted from your shoulders. You seem happier and more fulfilled. What happened?"

"I will not lie. For months after we broke up I was miserable and moped around a lot. But one morning I woke up and decided I did not want to be sad anymore. I did not want to depend on anybody for my external happiness anymore. Because if I had let someone get in my head again, I would fall into old habits and that was not the life I wanted to live. Instead of living for work and women, I decided to quit my job and start working out. That morning I got to work and finished things I needed to do. I met Ken Winters, so that was cool."

"Wait, hold on a sec, you met Ken Winters?"

"Yea, he's surprisingly down to earth. A great conversationalist and I think he bought your first piece. He called it breathtaking. I really did not know that you could do it, but even when we're apart, you can still prove me wrong. Anyway, to continue with my story, the next morning I just ran and I ran. I stopped to catch my breath once I reached the capital. I turned around and looked out at the city. Seeing the whole picture instead of just part of it. For the first time since I moved here, I saw its true beauty. I saw all the care and consideration of the thousands of people that built this city and the people who work each day to make this city their home. Every day I felt hope. Hope was something I did not experience since before my father left. I thought I had hope for you, but I realized it was a temporary fix. I realized I had to find happiness for myself and by myself, that all the money and women in the world could not make me happy. That was something I'd need to discover on my own while depending on several true teammates. I soon got my dream job, the same job I was terrified of taking when I was younger because young Jack needed the world to cure him. I found a reason to be happy that is internal. I am working my dream job helping others to find their way, and I have you to thank for it, because if it were not for you, I would not know where to look."

"Wow, he really called it breathtaking. That is a three-syllable compliment from my favorite author!"

"Yes, he did, and I believe him. Also, ouch, I came to this huge realization and all you get out of it is the compliment of your art."

"You tend to rant a lot, and you know I can't resist a compliment about something I've accomplished."

"Fair enough. I will tell you I missed us."

"Me too."

Sarah smiles as the two embrace. They go back to dancing as Jack hears what song is playing.

"Sarah."

Sarah looks at Jack curiously as he gladly announces softly to Sarah.

"This is our song."

Sarah listens to the melancholic melody and smiles as she remembers their first date when they declared this to be their song. They look each other, swaying in silence as they just listen to their song until it ends.

The rest of the night goes by quickly as the two spend the night catching each other up on their lives. They laugh and talk as if they've never separated. When the night was reaching its end, they part ways, knowing this would not be the last time they see each other.

Jack kept his promise to Sarah and starts writing to her back on their schedule until six months pass, and he receives a letter from Sarah unlike the rest.

35

SHOULD I TELL HIM?

May 04
Dear Jack,

I love hearing about the passion you have in your job. That is clearly visible by the way you write about it. And to answer your question, I am so excited to be graduating at the end of the month. As for what I am going to do with my degree? I already have job offers from several art galleries, quite a few here in California, and one from Salt Lake City! And I am happy to be doing something that I will absolutely love. This week has been as eventful as any last week could be, you know, cramming for finals and preparing for graduation. You know, school stuff. I am not sure if I should tell you this, but I know in my heart that I should tell you. Jeremy and I broke up last week. It was weird because he was the first guy to break up with me. Normally I do the breaking up. Do not worry about me. I am okay with it. I feel quite relieved and hope that does not make me a bad person. Does it? I already know what you are going to say, so you do not need to say it. You would say something like it was because you never loved him. Although you would use bigger words or poetic language. Jack, I must tell you I love getting your letters twice a month. They are the highlight of my day when I get them because they remind me of home. A little of me believes why I did not mind when Jeremy broke up with me was because of your letters. Sorry if that makes it sound like it was your fault because it was not. Anyway, I miss you, and I wonder sometimes if you think of me as much as I think of you.

Love always,
Sarah

For two weeks, Jack fell silent, not responding to Sarah. It's like he became a ghost. Sarah grew anxious waiting in his radio silence until one stormy night while looking out the window, she hears a tap. She investigates the cause of the noise and sees Jack out front throwing pebbles at her window. She rushes down the stairs bursting through the front door and yelling out, "Jack!"

36

— · —

DRENCHED IN RAIN

Jack stands in front of Sarah's apartment in the pouring rain holding the letter that has been transformed to mush by the water. Sarah stands, looking at the drenched man. "Jack, why are you here?"

Jack presents the sopping wet letter in his hands as he explains.

"I have read this letter over and over for two weeks interpreting its meaning, until I could not take it anymore. The one conclusion I thought of after reading it over and over was the fact that I had to see you."

Sarah moves into Jack's arms. It felt right having Sarah in his arms. He stands watching as the rain distorts her hair. He looks into her eyes, watching her face glisten under the streetlight. They were drenched.

"Wow, you're soaked. Come up the stairs. I'll get you out of those clothes. Come to my bedroom."

Jack smiles and raises one eyebrow, as Sarah defensively states, "That is not what I meant, pervert. You came all this way. I don't want you to catch a cold. I have clothes you can wear."

Jack nods as they both head up the stairs to her bedroom, while Sarah goes to get Jack a towel to dry himself off. As he is waiting he notices a painting on the wall. It is a more complete version of a painting she had in her old apartment. The tree on the painting is the same, but she has added a plethora of other things. The painting now has a lot of blue and green with a giant oak tree front and center. The tree is in full bloom with the silhouettes of a man and a woman holding hands. The woman has a crimson red heart sitting on her chest. The male silhouette has a lime green brain on his head. Over the couple is an archway of music notes and different colored swirls and flowers. On one branch of the tree stands a single pure white apple shining above the couple. The whole painting is done well with each brush stroke methodically placed. Jack sits there admiring the painting, thinking of what it could mean, and why he never truly realized Sarah's potential as an artist.

Sarah came to Jack with a pink towel and a T-shirt. "I hope you do not mind that the towel is pink and I brought my ex's shirt. You can wear it while I dry your shirt and jacket."

"Ah, yes."

"Here you go."

Jack takes his jacket and his shirt off, handing them to Sarah. She gapes at Jack's chiseled new body. His shoulders are broad, squared by a perfectly full and sculpted chest with six-pack abs that tapered off into a V. He has got an Adonis-like body with every muscle on his upper torso prominent and sculpted, leaving Sarah speechless for a second.

"Um, excuse me, mister, when were you going to tell me you have muscles?"

Jack trades his wet clothes for the towel and shirt as he dries himself off.

"First, I've always had muscles. It's how I move and stuff. Second, a couple of years ago I started working out and cleaned up my diet. I gave up drinking and women so I needed other vices."

"Sure, you come here looking like a superhero and tell me it's no big deal. Whatever, I'll start your laundry."

Sarah takes one more look at Jack and walks down stairs as Jack pulls an envelope out of his back pocket and puts it on the desk as he puts on the shirt Sarah gave him. It's two sizes too big for him and the front has a kitten wearing headphones with a tie-dye background. It is not his regular style but he thought it was better than nothing. He spread his arms out, flapping all the extra fabric around like a child wearing his dad's shirt. Sarah comes back to Jack playing with his oversized shirt and laughs at him. She sits in silence for a while until she clears her throat.

"Having fun?"

"This guy was huge. You said he was a bigger version of Tim, not that he was three of Tim put together."

"I do not judge the men I date by their stature."

"Sure, good to know," Jack says as he points to the painting. "I see you finished the painting?"

"Yeah, I had an artist block, but when we stopped dating I had a burst of inspiration. I call it hearts and minds."

"Wow, it is beautiful. You're good, kid."

"Oh, golly, mister, you think I could make it to the big leagues someday?"

"Well, if you keep doing masterpieces like this, you can reach the stars!" Jack says in an old-time announcer's voice as both laugh and catch each other's eyes.

Sarah finally asks, "Jack, why are you here?"

Jack grabs Sarah by the hips and brushes her hair out of her face as he kisses her. "Because I can't write that in a letter."

"Not with that attitude you can't. But why?"

"The real reason was because I have something I wanted to give you in person."

"Oh yeah, what is that?"

Jack grabs the envelope off the desk, showing Sarah as he expounds. "Sarah, in this envelope there are two plane tickets for after you graduate. I want you to come back to Salt Lake. One ticket is from here to Salt Lake and the other is from Salt Lake to here. In my heart of hearts, I hope you don't use the second ticket, but it is up to you."

"Jack, I don't..."

"Shh, don't answer right now. Take some time to think about it. In the meantime, how long do my clothes have to dry?"

"Well, they were wet. I'd give them an hour."

"So, I've only got an hour. That's too bad."

Jack walks away while Sarah grabs his arm.

"But my roommate does not come home for the next few hours, you can stay till then!"

"Oh, you don't say. What will we do with the remaining time?"

Sarah takes off her shirt, revealing a purple laced bra he wants to see on the floor immediately. Her body's perfect and smooth and it is just like seeing it for the first time. She strokes the sheets, beckoning for him to join her. He reaches out feeling for the grooves in her hips. "Cuddle?" she whispers, answering the joke her body made him forget he just made.

Jack smiles as he takes off his shirt and starts kissing Sarah passionately.

37

— ⋅ —

BACK TO THE BEGINNING

<u>A few months later</u>

Sarah sits on a plane leaving San Francisco. Jack got her a window seat and she spends the flight looking for the familiar landscape of Salt Lake. She gets lost in her thoughts thinking about the night she and Jack had a couple of months ago. Jack was silent until she told him she would visit Salt Lake. His only response was to say that he was looking forward to it. She wonders what it is he wants her to see in Salt Lake. Once she lands, she runs toward the entrance and sees Tim with his wife, shocked to see Jack is nowhere to be found. She frowns and tries to hide her disappointment, as she sheepishly queries, "Hey Tim, how are you?"

Tim, with a big grin on his face, riles Sarah to get a smile out of her. "Is that any way to talk to your true love who is now leagues above you? It's okay, I forgive you. I'm off the market, which I can see clearly makes you miserable, but I'm doing awesome!"

Sarah smirks as she knows what is happening. "Oh, I see you still have delusions of the fact that you have ever had a shot with me."

"That dress makes you look fat, or did you just put on some depression weight for not having me!"

"Don't make me puke. Besides the fat I can lose, you can never lose that ugly of yours!"

Both stare at each other like they were squaring off in a boxing match, and Stephanie is about to step in until both burst into laughter. And once the storm settles, Sarah finally asks, "Hey, where is Jack?"

Tim looks at Stephanie, who gives an approving nod.

"Jack is not here, but he's got the day planned out already. He wants to make it special for you. So while he prepares your big day, you will spend the afternoon with us at our place where you will get changed, drop your stuff off, et cetera. Then at five, Jack will pick you up and that is all I can tell you about tonight."

"Do any of you still live in the same apartment?"

"Oh, I can answer that. Six months ago that place got shut down. They finished demolishing it a few months ago. Jack now lives in a one bedroom downtown and we moved to a little house in the west valley, so some things have changed." Tim glances at his watch and grabs Sarah's bag. "Okay we should get going so we have time for you to shower, stinky."

Sarah gives Tim an annoyed look as he and his wife leave and just as they turn their back, she smells her shoulder and follows.

Tim is driving and Stephanie is holding his hand as the two smile looking at the road ahead. They sit in silence for the first half of the trip, only listening to the radio softly playing in the background. It is very uncharacteristic of Tim to be silent for over five minutes so she attempts to break the silence. "So, anything new with you two?"

Tim glances at Stephanie, who nods. "I still work at my job. As you know, I took Jack's spot when he left and Steph is busy taking care of a small child growing inside of her as we speak."

"Wait, Stephanie, you're pregnant? Congratulations!"

Steph looks in shock as she gasps in a sarcastic tone. "Wait a second, I'm pregnant? Nobody told me that. Babe, why did you not tell me I'm pregnant? Who's the other girl?"

"I'm so sorry, sweetheart. I forgot to tell you I slept with you and one day out of nowhere, boom, there's a baby!"

Both laugh, pleased with themselves as Sarah crosses her arms. "All right, you two don't need to be jerks about it! You know what? Silence is better!"

Sarah pouts in the back as the two laugh and drive until they park in front of a small one-story yellow house and Tim announces, "Okay, we are here. I'll get your bag."

The day goes by quickly as she sits there contemplating their entire relationship. She remembers flowers just because it was Monday and when Jack would whisper nonsense in her ear calling them sweet nothings, or when he would grab her hand leading them to a place he was excited to show her. She also remembers the last time he traveled to San Francisco in the pouring rain. This makes her even more excited for five o'clock to arrive.

38

WHO ASKED YOU?

<u>Three months earlier</u>

Tim meets Jack at a torn-down building and they stand by a truck as Tim talks. "You know of all the places you would ask me to meet for life advice, I never thought it would be in front of our old apartment complex."

"They are going to finish demolishing this building tomorrow so I thought I'd grab some things."

"Jack, you are a strange man, but while I have you here, I got to let you know Stephanie is pregnant!"

"That is great news, man. I'm happy for you!"

Both men embrace and Tim starts a story.

"You know, when I married Stephanie, I thought to myself I never thought she could get more beautiful, but now that she's pregnant, she's even more beautiful. The future mother of my child! She became even more gorgeous to me. You know when I was single, I thought to myself that life did not get better than this, but I was wrong. It gets better every time I look at Stephanie."

"Tim, that is a wonderful sentiment, but I did not actually call you over for life advice. I need a hand with something."

Jack goes to the back of the truck and lifts a tarp, revealing several pieces of concrete from the building.

"We may also need some more guys and some power tools."

<u>Present day</u>

Jack starts out his day the same way he normally would by waking up and running to the gym. After eating a healthy breakfast he runs out of his apartment where he sees a group of men and he smiles.

"Ready, boys?"

The men nod as Jack hops in the truck and they drive to a park where they put together slabs of concrete that have been shaped like a giant puzzle. After hours of placing the slabs in the appropriate arrangement, Jack looks at his creation with pride, when his phone rings.

"Hey, Tim—she did great. Okay, keep her busy until four. She can start getting ready then as long as she's ready by five o'clock sharp. I'll have the limo pick her up then. Tim, thank you. Goodbye."

Jack hangs up, telling the boys, "Great job men! Now let's go. Drinks on me!"

All the men cheer as Jack peers back at the stage that is set up and smiles.

Later, back at Jack's apartment, he is getting dressed in a tuxedo. He puts his hands on his head, pacing back and forth, and starts talking to himself.

"What if all this is for nothing? What if she says no? I mean, it has been a while—no, I'm talking crazy. There is no way she will say no, we were together! Oh, damn, I put way too much money into this. What was I thinking? I do not make a lot of money anymore. I am crazy, that is the only explanation. Argh! Maybe I'm just over-analyzing this, what do you think?"

Jack turns to a small gray tabby cat wearing a little red bow who stares at Jack with curious green eyes. It lets out a tiny meow, then turns away looking for other things to occupy itself with.

"You're right. I'm overreacting and you're a fucking cat. I am going crazy."

39

— • —

DUCKS

Back at Tim's house, Sarah exits the shower in a pink robe as she sees a white box with the words "Wear me" written in Jack's handwriting. Sarah opens the box, seeing something navy blue with a red bow and a small note written by Jack. She sits down on the bed, reading it.

Sarah,

I know right now you are sitting in your pink fluffy robe reading this and looking around to see if I'm in the room. I am not and I also know you brought with you two dresses for this occasion because you can't decide between the little black dress you wore to the opera or that little red number with the black stripe running down the side. Although either of those would be incredible choices, in this box I have the dress you eyeballed all those years ago and a red bow you can wear in your hair as a fascinator to tie the outfit together. I am glad that you are the same size because I bought this years ago. As soon as you said you liked it and were saving it for a special occasion, I knew I had to buy it for you. I am happy I finally get to see this on you. Anyway, I will keep this brief so you can finish getting ready. I'll see you at five o'clock sharp.

Love always,

Jack

Sarah examines the dress and smiles. As she finishes getting ready she remembers when they went to the mall and she spotted this dress. At five o'clock she steps out in the mid-length sapphire blue strapless dress with a slit on the side of the leg. It fits her silhouette perfectly. She accented it with a silver necklace and bracelet and has the red bow in her hair. She smiles as a limo pulls up and the driver opens the door for her. She is surprised to not see Jack. As they take off, she asks the driver, "Where's Jack?"

The driver smiles as he peers in the rearview mirror and answers, "Waiting!" He then closes the privacy window as he drives away. When they reach the gate of the park, Sarah realizes this is the same park they went to on their first date. The driver opens the door and hands her a blindfold. "We are here. Please put this on!"

Sarah nods and puts the blindfold on. The driver leads her away until a familiar hand grabs her and steers her several steps into the park. The hand lets go of hers and removes the blindfold. She sees Jack in a blue tuxedo with a red bowtie, smiling. "Look closer!"

She then notices what Jack has done, and she tears up not believing what she's seeing. "How?" Jack lets Sarah take in the sights before he explains this simple yet elaborate sight. Four long white poles surrounding this concrete structure have created a canopy of white lights. The concrete is crudely cut but noticeably shaped into a heart. It looks like it has taken someone days to smooth out and shape it. The heart is roughly the size of a small stage that could fit a dozen people comfortably. In the middle lays a small table with two chairs. A long tablecloth flows down to the ground and on the top is a bottle of wine, two glasses, and a tray covered with a silver lid. Sarah starts to tear up as she gently whimpers, "Jack!"

Jack smiles as he wipes away her tears. Sarah kisses Jack before he leads her to the table. "Dinner?" Jack pulls out Sarah's chair and subtly unties his shoe as they eat. "The sushi and the limo were the easy parts. All that took was timing and money. The lights and poles were also easy to obtain. They are just metal poles and Christmas lights. I have them plugged into a tiny generator that I got with everything else at the hardware store. But when it comes to the concrete we are sitting on...guess where it came from?"

Sarah takes a stab and answers with an educated guess. "If I had to wager a guess, I would say the theme is things that have to do with our first date, other than the clothing and the limo which are just red herrings to throw me off your scent. This park and sushi are part of our first date. You did not include the ice rink for obvious reasons. But this concrete is throwing me, so I can't guess what it is."

Jack laughs and kisses Sarah's hand. "Impressive. You picked out the red herrings and the theme. All of it represents of our firsts; our first date, our first kiss, our first time we said I love you, and most importantly, where I was standing the first time I met you!"

Sarah looks at the ground in shock and looks up at Jack. "Are you saying this is…?"

"Exactly!"

Jack smiles as he takes her hands and says, "This park also has another first. It is the first time I thought there had to be more to life than the way I was living it. On the day I met you, I was at the park a few blocks away watching two ducks frolic and play in the water, living their life without worry or care. I thought to myself, ducks can fly, yet they choose to spend their time in water because that's what they love to do. I wondered if I would ever love what I do. Coincidently, later that day I met you and my life changed. You showed me life is more than just a gray area, and I, too, could fly and land in a spot I love in my life if I had you. Not only did you show me a path that I wanted to be on, but you also showed me how I could grow hope, and this hope slowly grew and developed into love. I have always thought love was something that was made up by people who wrote books and movies for their financial gain, but you showed me that love is real. Love is time I spend with you. Love is all the moments I held your hand or gave you flowers. Love is the hope you gave me to chase my dreams. Love is you and me always. And this was something I did not realize until you left, but now your back and I remember what love is, and why I was enamored by ducks. I want you to be my duck--that last part was lame. I guess what I'm trying to say is, Sarah, I love you, always, and I knew that from the time I saw you back when this concrete was still on the roof were I first met you."

Sarah was speechless, both because of Jack's strong declaration of love and the extent he went to show her that love. She sits there as the two grasp each other's hands. She leans over and kisses him, not knowing what words could counter his. As the two are kissing, she identifies something soft brush on her feet and suddenly she jumps up and screams. "Jack, what is that!"

Jack has to think for a second. He laughs as he grabs the little gray cat with the red bow and presents it to Sarah. Jack stands up as he removes something silver and shiny from the cat's bow and puts the cat back down on his leash. Suddenly, their song plays from a distance. Tim, Stephanie, Cliff, Ruth, and Julie come into view filming as Jack gets down on one knee.

"Sarah, I love you and that will never change." Jack presents a silver ring with a sizable diamond and Sarah grows bright red in surprise as their friends look on with excitement and Jack, on one knee, asks, "Sarah Reeding, will you marry me?"

Epilogue

In a two-story house framed by two oak trees and a white picket fence with an exquisite lawn, lie an aged couple with silver hair. They are inside their house of many decades, decorated with framed photos of their family of four. They gaze into each other's eyes as they grab each other's left hands with their matching golden bands. The man leans toward his wife and whispers to her, "That was one hell of a ride!"

The End

AFTERWORD

Thank you so much for purchasing and reading this book. If you enjoyed or read this book out of spite, please leave a review on amazon or any relevant site. Thank you again for your support and hope that you find my books in the future. I could not do this without you, I wish you the best.

Acknowledgments

This Book has been a real labor of love for the past six years. Thanks to those that never doubted.

I would like to acknowledge everyone who had a hand in editing this book. India, Rozi, Tiffany, Sandra, and Gen provided by Reedsy, Fiver, and small favors. Without them, this novel would be nowhere close to readable or put together as it has become. Thank you, you're truly angels.

Thanks to the cover designer whose work was incredible and better than I could have imagined.

Thank you to all the friends and family who supported me throughout this journey, and then putting up with my only conversation being this book, you're the best teammates I could ask for.

And Last but not least I would like to thank my dad. He showed me the impact books can have on my life, without the influence of reading a good book, I would have never been willing to write one.

ALSO BY

John Orrick is a story of a psychopath that killed young boys for sport, it is not for thee light of heart. With that being said, enjoy the preview.

Chapter 1:
Run

The child's run turned to a sprint; his steps gradually slowed as the chilly winter night gradually introduced itself into the boys' lungs. With a croak in his voice, he screamed for help, to no avail. Because to him his worst nightmare was chasing him with long legs, his strides were larger than the boys. From the shadows, the tall, intimidating figure of John Orrick stepped into the light, flickering in and out. He was well dressed and stepped like he was gliding. The boy saw the glimmer of rounded spectacles and the flash of crooked teeth reveal themselves as he mocked the boy. His black attire and top hat towered over any man. No doubt to the boy John was a monster who lured him in with false promises just to frighten the boy with his long-gloved fingers reaching for his throat. The chase brought a light to his dark brown eyes. "Little boy!" John called out in a singsong voice, not out of breath. The boy was running for his life. "Tiny boy!" he called out again. The boy ran himself into one of the stone lain alleyways with less light than the streetlamps provided, hoping to provide himself with some shelter, but the snow was fresh and so were the footprints the boy left behind. Soon the boy was cowering in a corner as Orrick towered over him, smiling his crooked smile, adjusting his spectacles. "Runaway, far away," he says, laughing. "Try to hide." He broke off a dangling icicle from the building. "Nothing you try will matter because I always get my boy!" violently he jabbed the icicle into the boy's neck, causing the boy to fall to the ground instantly dead. "Timothy, clean up this mess, you have ten minutes before the police arrive. The boys' screams were soft toward the end, but he caused enough of a fuss to alert someone." John said, wiping blood from his spectacles. "Right away Mr. Orrick." I said as I came out of the corner, I was hiding in order to not alert the victim of a second's presence.

"Very well, I'll be waiting in the mansion when you are done, leave no evidence." John put his spectacles back on and disappeared into the shadows.

I went up to the boy adorning my own gloves after checking the boy's pulse. Sure enough, he was dead on impact. This was a brutal murder, but not Orrick's worst. The boy was no older than eight years old. He had clean blonde hair and newer laced boots; it was clear from the clothing he came from wealth. I turned the boy over on his back so the blood could flow evenly into the streets. I cleaned off any evidence of another person being involved. Once I removed the icicle, the blood spilled out into the alleyway. By morning, the body would be buried in snow, but the police officers will prevent that. Body disposal was not my problem. All I had to do was make sure nothing could point to Orrick. As I left, I walked backward, wiping any remaining footprints with my coat. Once I got to the spot where the chase started, I heard the whistle of the officers as they marched to the crime scene. Being far enough away, I adorned my coat and headed up the hill to Orrick's mansion.

Orrick manor was massive with gothic influence. It was spacious, yet never full. The floor was adorned with red and black rugs in a classic pattern, it only distracted from the dark burgundy wood that was all over and was always perfect with walls looking like they would form to a point, and a zigzagged stairway that led to the bedrooms, he had red and black chairs that matched the rug in the entryway. With some plain art of horses, and flowers, and roman statues, because the surname Orrick was of roman origin. Orrick kept a few family maids to clean the place, but they were not allowed into his basement. He kept a prison and his study there. I never saw him use the cage, but he told me he used to use it. After a kill, he always stayed in the basement. I used my key to walk down the grey basement, going down an old wooden staircase. I saw Orrick in his study lit by a single lantern highlighting him and the thick stonework that adorned the walls. He was deep in concentration, his hat and coat on the rack. He was still in his black tweed suit trousers and starched white shirt, kept crisp and starched. His coat was big enough to shield him from splatter. I grabbed some wood and threw it in the fireplace. That I found by memory and started a fire illuminating his pale face even more. "Is the Job done Timothy." He said without looking up from his maps.

"Yes, Sir."

"Very well, thanks for the fire, Timothy. Your excused."

"Sir, have you had supper yet?"

John looked at me with curiosity. "I'm not hungry."

"Sir, eat, especially with the energy you expounded tonight."

"I barely went on a jot Timothy," he said plainly, I stood there until he relented "fine you can deliver my supper, as long as you also eat."

"Yes, sir." I said excitedly and as I approached the stairs, I remembered a rumor and turned to John. "Oh, one more thing. Have you heard the rumors, Mr. Orrick?"

"Rumors?" Orrick took off his spectacles, giving me his attention.

"I've heard whispers of a detective because of the recent murder sprees of the upper class. They sent a high-profile detective from Spain to investigate."

"Don't be a coward Timothy, you can say because of my murders."

"Yes, sir but-"

"But nothing, you should know by now, we can talk openly about the murders. What I am doing is a benefit."

"It's not that, Mr. Orrick, it's just if this man is as good as they say, well, we may not continue as we are."

"Nonsense!" John said with a chuckle. "My downfall will never be at the hands of a Spaniard."

"Ok, just tread lightly Sir, I can't lose you."

"Timothy, nothing is going to happen to me. Now go, I'm hungry now." He said, shooing me away. "If you are worried, check the crime scene tomorrow, I also heard whispers. He is said to be arriving early morning, you can tell me your findings then." John went back to his studies, and I hurried up the stairs.

The next morning, I went back to see a crowd of spectators to see the detective in action. Detective Antonio Fernandez was an interesting fellow who had put on a show. He was smaller than a man from England, but he made up his height with tall black boots that went up to the knee of starch white trousers. His over coat had a long tail on the back like a pianist would adorn for a concert. Both his coat and vest were scarlet. Probably why he was known as the scarlet detective. He tipped his black top hat as he smiled, shaping his sharp face; he had a thin, curled mustache attached to a thin pointed beard, his cheeks and neck naked. His eyes were a lighter brown than Johns. This man was Orrick's antithesis, Whereas John was quiet and calculated this man was loud and loved to put on a show, with a gaudy attire and open body language. He may not need to be competent; his loudness could cause a threat. "Ladies and gentlemen of White Chapple London. As you can see, I am not like you. My skin is bronze while yours is ivory and brown. My English sounds foreign to you, but I have no accent. You do." Antonio said in jest as the crowd laughed. "Anyhow, I am not here to point out our differences, but I am here to relieve your pain." He looked around. "I know you are wondering what that means. Well, let's look back to 1888. Seven years ago, there was a madman who killed five of earth's loveliest creatures. The fairer of our race, women. Now there is another madman in this the year of our lord 1895. And this man is not going after women but children, and he has slaughtered twenty innocent souls." He puts his hat on his chest, bowing. "But no more. I vow to stop this man! I have solved ninety-nine cases and this murder of little boys will be my number one hundred!" he raised his arms and the spectators cheered, it was like they were watching a show and not the grim murder scene behind him.

To be continued.

The Novel Smash Ball was supposed to be the next novel ready but right now, after finishing this book I learned a lot of the mistakes I made in this book were also in smash ball, so I wrote John Orrick for NaNoWriMo. John Orrick will be ready sooner than Smash Ball, it will also be a self-edit, were as I hope to query for Smash Ball when it's ready. John Orrick will be out by the end of this year and with any luck, Smash Ball will be ready by the beginning of next year. For those that made it to this point, thank you for your support.

ABOUT AUTHOR

 Nyk Brownsilva is an adult contemporary romance author. His educational background is in business and psychology, and his professional background is in customer service. This has given him a deep understanding of human relationships and the way people work with each other that makes his writing come alive with rich, relatable characters and compelling plots. Nyk's true passion lies in writing, and he is excited to delve deeper into this world and share meaningful stories with his readers. Nyk's previous works have included two romance short stories entitled *Idiots in Love* and *Unplugged*. Nyk's debut novel is *The Roof*, a boy meets girl adult contemporary romance. With his gift for storytelling and his deep understanding of the human heart, Nyk's works will captivate readers and leave them wanting more.